FROM THE
NANCY DREW FILES

THE CASE: Nancy checks out a series of death threats against Chicago's hottest young designer.

CONTACT: Teen fashion sensation Kim Daley calls Nancy for help against industrial spies—and cold-blooded killers.

SUSPECTS: Morgan Daley—Kim's mousy sister has good reason to hate her arrogant sibling.

Paul Lavalle—the handsome fashion photographer is still in love with Kim, but she keeps brushing him off.

Lina Roccocini—Kim's archrival is jealous of her success and wants Paul for herself.

COMPLICATIONS: Nancy is poisoned and has only seventy-two hours to find the killer—and a life-saving antidote!

Books in THE NANCY DREW FILES ™ Series

Available from ARCHWAY Paperbacks

THE NANCY DREW FILES CASE · 30

DEATH BY DESIGN

Carolyn Keene

AN ARCHWAY PAPERBACK
Published by POCKET BOOKS

New York   London   Toronto   Sydney   Tokyo

AN ARCHWAY PAPERBACK *Original*

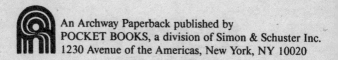

An Archway Paperback published by
POCKET BOOKS, a division of Simon & Schuster Inc.
1230 Avenue of the Americas, New York, NY 10020

Copyright © 1988 by Simon & Schuster Inc.
Cover art copyright © 1988 Jim Mathewuse
Produced by Mega-Books of New York, Inc.

ISBN: 0-671-64697-4

First Archway Paperback printing December 1988

10 9 8 7 6 5 4 3 2 1

Printed in the U.S.A.

IL 7+

DEATH BY DESIGN

Chapter

One

BUT, NED, I'm only going to be gone for a week!" Nancy Drew protested. "You don't really mind, do you?"

It was nine o'clock on a cold, gray November morning, and Nancy was just about to leave for Chicago. She cast a worried glance at her boyfriend, Ned Nickerson, who was slumped down next to her on the living-room sofa. Ned's only answer was a mournful sigh.

"Ned, I've never seen you like this!" Nancy said. "I can't believe you're so upset!"

Ned sighed again, and then abruptly straightened up. The corners of his mouth were quivering as if he were about to break into a smile.

"I'm just teasing you. Of course I don't mind," he said. "I mean, I *mind,* but I understand. But since it's for a case, I'll let you go this once. I will miss you, though," he added softly, slipping his arm around Nancy's shoulder and pulling her close.

"You really had me going for a minute there!" Nancy lay her head against his shoulder. "I'm going to miss you, too," she said, lifting her head for a quick kiss.

"It's horrible that all this had to come up when you've got a week off." Ned was home from Emerson College for a brief vacation. He'd come over to drive Nancy to the train station. "But at least this case should be interesting. I don't usually get the chance to hobnob with the stars of the fashion world."

"How'd you get the chance to do it this time?" Ned asked. "Have you started advertising on TV?"

Nancy laughed. "Not yet. You can thank George for this one." George Fayne was one of Nancy's two best friends. "When she went to Chicago last week to watch those skating finals, she met Kim Daley. I don't know if you've ever heard of Kim—"

"The fashion designer?" Ned asked.

"That's the one."

"You don't wear her clothes, do you?"

"They're too expensive for me. Besides, it's not my style. You know—everything's huge, with shoulders padded out to *here.*" Nancy held her hands out three inches from her shoulders. "Kim once designed a whole line of leather skirts that you could lengthen or shorten by zipping on attachments. There were even some boots you could attach. I mean, it's great stuff to look at—on someone else. But it's not the kind of thing you'd wear every day.

"Anyway," Nancy continued, "Kim made a costume for one of the skaters, and she was sitting right next to George. Kim started telling George all about some mysterious death threats she'd been getting on the phone—and pretty soon George had persuaded her to call me.

"Kim needs me right away, too," Nancy continued. "She wants me to find out who's threatening her—and to stop them—before her big summer preview. She's going to be one of several designers in a huge show in just a few days. Kim's the main attraction, and the show could really make her reputation internationally."

"Well, don't have dinner with anyone but Bess while you're there," Ned ordered. Nancy's other best friend, Bess Marvin, was going to Chicago with her. George was on a sailing trip in the Caribbean. "And keep away from those big-city guys. I know how impressionable you are."

Nancy picked up a throw pillow and whacked

3

Ned over the head with it. "Hey! Do I lecture *you* about all those gorgeous cheerleaders at college?"

The doorbell rang before Ned could answer. "Door's open, Bess," Nancy called. "Come on in."

Bess Marvin pushed open the front door and rushed into the living room, her blond hair peeking out of her soft pink beret. "Are you ready?" she asked, not waiting for a reply. "Let's get to the train station before I think of anything else I forgot!"

"I'll load the car, Nan," Ned said.

Ned and Bess headed out the front door, and Nancy walked to the bottom of the stairs.

"Dad! Hannah! I'm leaving!" she called. "Come say goodbye!" In a second her father came down the stairs, followed by the Drews' housekeeper, Hannah Gruen.

"This house is going to be much too quiet with the two of you gone! I don't know what I'll do with myself," Hannah complained.

Nancy grinned. "Just empty out the freezer so it'll hold all those tons of fish Dad's going to bring home. Are *you* packed, Dad?"

Carson Drew's law practice kept him so busy that he almost never found the time to take a vacation. Now, at last, he was getting a holiday—a long-awaited fishing trip in Canada.

He smiled back at Nancy. "I'm getting there. Fishing rod's in the car, anyway." Then he grew serious. "I just wish there was some way you could get ahold of me if you need me, Nancy. If I'd known you'd be on a case, I'd have chosen to stay someplace with a phone—not a log cabin in the middle of nowhere!"

"But a phone would scare away all the fish!" Nancy said. She gave him a quick hug. "Don't worry about me, Dad. I'll be fine."

"And you'll call me if there's anything wrong, won't you?" Hannah put in anxiously.

"Of course I will. But nothing's going to go wrong." Just then Ned came back. "Bess is ready and rarin' to go," he said.

"Then you'd better get going, Nan," said her father. "Come on, Hannah. I'll never finish packing if you don't help me."

Nancy was grateful her father was giving her the chance to be alone with Ned for a minute before she left.

"Brrrr! What a day!" Bess said more than an hour later as a blast of cold air shook the taxi she and Nancy were riding in. To their left lay the vast grayness of Lake Michigan. Above them, the sky was a sullen mass of November clouds.

"Once we get to the hotel I'm staying inside," Bess continued. "That wind's not going to mess up my hair."

"Bess, we're going to *see* a fashion preview. Not be in it!"

"I know, but maybe someone'll discover me and make me a model," Bess said. She sneaked a glance at her reflection in the rearview mirror. "If I lose enough weight, I mean—"

"Stranger things have happened," replied Nancy, suppressing a grin.

"Oh, there's our hotel," Bess said.

When she'd first talked to Kim Daley, Nancy was surprised that Kim had chosen the Hamilton Hotel to set up her temporary showroom. True, the Hamilton was the site of the fashion preview, and it was one of Chicago's most elegant hotels —but it was also one of its stuffiest. Why, Nancy had wondered, would a young fashion designer set up her offices there?

Nancy found out why after she and Bess entered the lobby to register. The hotel had the tightest security she'd ever seen. She and Bess even had to carry passes identifying them as Kim Daley's guests.

"To stop any unauthorized person from seeing her designs before the show," the check-in clerk explained. "It's difficult for us to keep track of everyone, as you might imagine. The passes help."

Nancy nodded sympathetically. "Kim is staying here, isn't she?"

"Oh, yes. She's set up a temporary office and showroom on the thirtieth floor. In fact, as soon as you've settled in, she wants to take you to lunch."

"Settled in?" Bess glanced around the Hamilton's beautiful lobby with its pale apricot-colored marble walls and lush Oriental rugs. "If our room is as gorgeous as this lobby, I just might move in."

An hour later Nancy and Bess were leaving their suite—which *was* gorgeous but now littered with the outfits Bess had tried on and rejected—and heading for the elevator.

There were two people going up in the elevator already. One was a chubby man about five foot seven who appeared to be in his late twenties, wearing a double-breasted gray suit, black tie, and black alligator loafers. The other was a woman in her fifties with a pile of brassy blond hair. Her figure was matchstick thin, and her leopard-print minidress and huge claw-shaped earrings looked much too young for her.

"He told me Kim was a total slave driver," she was saying in a raspy voice. Probably a chainsmoker, Nancy decided. She had barely glanced at the girls as they stepped into the elevator. "Half her staff's quit already."

"I've heard that, too," answered the woman's companion. "Kim's all smiles for the press, but when no one's around . . . It's no wonder she has so many enemies."

Enemies! Nancy darted a look at Bess. Her friend's face was blank, but Nancy could tell that Bess was listening.

"Well, she's never been too smiley when *I've* been around," the woman complained. "I just can't stand— Oh, here's the thirtieth floor."

As the doors slid open, the woman seemed startled that Nancy and Bess were getting off at the same floor. But she quickly recovered and swept down the hall ahead of them.

At the end of the hall the brassy-haired woman jabbed the bell with her thumb, and instantly a heavyset security guard opened the door.

"May I help you?" he asked in a rumbling bass voice.

"My name is Louella Teasdale," the woman announced, "and this is Oscar Davis, my assistant. We're here to see Kim."

"A Ms. Teasdale and a Mr. Davis?" the guard asked the receptionist at a desk behind him. The receptionist scanned her appointment book, then shook her head.

"Sorry," said the guard. "You'll have to call for an appointment."

"But—but Kim knows us!" sputtered the chubby young man. "We're with *Fashion* magazine!"

Suddenly Nancy remembered where she'd heard Louella Teasdale's name before. She was *Fashion's* gossip columnist, and everyone in the fashion world paid attention to the magazine and her. Nancy didn't read it often—but no one who'd read it even once could forget Louella Teasdale's column. Her writing was unbelievably nasty—and sometimes clever. Was Ms. Teasdale planning a column on Kim?

The guard didn't seem to care what magazine she was with. He shook his head again.

"Kim Daley has never refused to see me!" declared the columnist huffily. "And she's never needed protection before, either. What's going on?"

The guard stared straight through her. "I don't know, ma'am."

For a second Ms. Teasdale looked as if she were about to storm past him, but then reconsidered and drew up her shoulders. "Come along, Oscar. Something very strange is going on here."

She turned and strode away, followed by a perspiring Oscar, who was doing his best to keep up.

Nancy watched their determined progress down the hall, then turned to the guard. "Hi. My name is Nancy Drew," she told him. "And this is my friend, Bess—"

"Marvin," interrupted the receptionist. "Go right in, girls. Ms. Daley is expecting you."

She waved the girls on past her desk and into instant chaos. The showroom was feverish with activity. Models were being pinned into sample dresses. Assistants were scurrying around with color swatches and fabric samples. In one corner a woman was frantically sewing black metallic trim onto a silver jumpsuit, and next to her a harassed-looking man was hanging finished dresses on long racks. And as background to all the activity was the pulsing beat of rock music blaring from hidden speakers.

Nancy and Bess threaded their way through the crowd. Passing a row of women sitting at sewing machines, they made their way to an office with Kim Daley's name on the door. As Nancy knocked, the door opened.

Kim's office was as chaotic as the showroom. What looked like hundreds of drawings were pinned to the walls, and the desk was buried in sketches, empty coffee cups, piles of fabric, and a box of cloth-covered buttons in every imaginable shade of pink. Nancy wondered how anyone got any work done.

"Nancy? Bess? Come on in. I'm Kim," said the woman behind the desk. She stood up abruptly, knocking a pile of zippers to the floor. "Who is who?"

"I'm Nancy, and this is Bess."

Kim Daley looked nothing like what Nancy had expected. She wore no makeup except for a smear of bright red lipstick, and she was dressed in black jeans, an oversize black sweatshirt, and sneakers. Her pitch black hair was short and combed forward, and she was wearing long earrings shaped like lobsters. Nancy smiled to herself. Here, she thought, was one of the great forces in teenage fashion—and who would know it?

"Nice to meet you both." Abruptly Kim jumped up from her desk and stuck her head into the workroom. "Sarah!" she shouted. "Could you come in here—right now?"

In a second a pale, skinny girl appeared. "We'd like some jasmine tea," Kim told her. "And could you find the rest of the cookies? *And* turn off that music? It's driving me crazy."

Sarah turned to leave—and almost tripped over a tiny Yorkshire terrier yapping its way in to greet Kim.

"And don't step on Chanel!" shouted Kim angrily. "That dog is worth two of you—at least!

"You might as well have a seat, girls," Kim continued. "Sarah will take forever. Now, listen a second." That's what we *were* doing! Nancy thought. "You've come just in time. I had another of those anonymous calls this morning. And if you don't stop them soon, I'm going to lose my mind!"

"We'll do everything we can," Nancy promised soothingly. "What did the caller say this time?"

"The usual. That if I don't look out I'll be colder than a department-store dummy, et cetera. The fashion industry is cutthroat, but this is ridiculous!" Kim's bright hazel eyes flashed both fear and anger.

"And you have absolutely no idea who the caller could be?" Nancy asked.

"Of course not! I mean, some people are jealous of me, which is understandable, but this is more than jealousy, isn't it? My staff's devoted to me. Even the press loves me. I haven't had a bad review yet."

Well, you certainly love yourself, thought Nancy, but I don't know if you're right about everyone else. Aloud, she asked, "What about Louella Teasdale?"

"Louella!" Kim exclaimed. *"You* haven't been talking to the press, have you?"

"Of course not," Nancy said evenly.

"Well, make sure you don't!" Kim snapped. "Please try to keep this as low-key as you can."

"We'll do our best," Nancy said.

"Nancy's very good at keeping things quiet," Bess put in loyally.

But Kim's eyes were on the door. "What can Sarah be doing—" Just then Sarah staggered in with a tray of tea and cookies. Nancy grinned as she watched Bess's eyes light up. As usual, Bess was about to decide to postpone the diet she was just about to start.

"Put it on my desk, Sarah," Kim ordered. Then her voice softened. "Chanel," she cooed. "Come up here, honey!"

From its spot under Kim's desk, the little dog stood up and jumped onto her lap.

"Want some tea, precious?" Kim crooned,

pouring some into her saucer. "And how about a cookie? I know these chocolate ones are your favorites." She plucked the largest cookie from the plate.

Beaming, Kim set the saucer of tea on the floor. Chanel sniffed at it and gave it a few dutiful laps before devouring the cookie. Nancy heard Bess stifle a giggle beside her.

"Now, where was I?" Kim asked, straightening up. "Oh, yes. About publicity—What is it *now,* Sarah?"

Sarah was awkwardly standing in the doorway with a sheaf of papers in her hands. She blushed. "I'm sorry, Kim. I need to get your approval on these—"

The phone on the desk rang. With a smothered groan Kim picked it up. "Kim Daley," she said in a crisp voice.

She listened for a second. Then her eyes widened with terror, and she clapped her hand over the mouthpiece. "It's them again!" she whispered, switching on the phone's speaker unit so Nancy and Bess could hear.

The voice at the other end was hideously distorted—a hissing, demented cackle like that of a voice in a nightmare.

"Say goodbye to your sweet life, Daley. You'll be dead by the end of the week. And this will show that I mean busines-s-s-s—"

An agonizingly shrill scream stabbed the air.

Bess doubled over, clutching her head in agony. Kim's little dog ran howling from the room. The scream grew louder—louder— And suddenly a huge crystal paperweight on Kim's desk exploded, shooting deadly shards of glass in every direction!

Chapter

Two

NANCY THREW HERSELF against Kim, pushing the designer down to the floor and protecting Kim with her body.

"My eye! I can't see!" Sarah screamed from the doorway a second later.

Nancy rushed to her. Sarah was doubled over, her hands covering her face. Gently Nancy lifted her hands away so she could see how badly Sarah had been hurt.

"Your eyes are okay," she said. "But it looks like a pretty deep cut just under the right one, though. Are there medical supplies here?"

Sarah shook her head.

"Bess, please take Sarah down to the lobby," Nancy said. "The hotel management should be able to help her."

Kim glared at Sarah, her face red with rage.

"Don't you tell them—or anyone—what happened!" she ordered. "It'll ruin my good name. And make sure you get back as fast as you can. We're busy."

Bess shot an indignant glance at Kim. Nancy was beginning to see why Kim had enemies. "Bess, are *you* all right?" Nancy asked before her friend could say anything to Kim.

"I think so," said Bess.

"Kim?" Nancy said, and Kim nodded her head yes.

"Good," said Nancy, running her fingers through her hair to check for shards of glass. "Then you two go down to the lobby."

Bess hurried Sarah out the door, and Nancy bent to pick up the pieces of glass that lay all over the floor.

"Oh, don't bother with that," said Kim carelessly. "I'll have my sister Morgan do it." There was a light knock at the door.

Nancy looked up to see a young woman of about nineteen poking her head around the open door.

"Are you all right, Kim?" asked the woman. "I heard a noise."

"I'm fine," said Kim impatiently, "or I will be

when Nancy gets to the bottom of all this. Nancy, my kid sister Morgan. Morgan, Nancy Drew— she's going to investigate those phone calls."

Kim's sister? As Nancy looked more closely, she began to see a resemblance. By anyone's standards Morgan was the prettier of the two— her warm chocolate eyes were thick-lashed and her dark hair curled softly around her shoulders. But her tense, strained expression and hunched-over posture made her look unattractive—the kind of person no one would ever look at twice. Nancy couldn't help feeling sorry for her.

"Hi, Morgan," she said warmly. "Want a cookie?"

"Oh, Morgan doesn't eat between meals," said Kim.

"Yes, I do," said Morgan. "It's just that I've been dieting. But, Kim, you haven't told me what that noise was. Is everything all right?"

"Everything's fine," Kim snapped. Nancy wondered why Kim was keeping her sister in the dark. "What do you have there? Do you want to show me something?" Kim went on.

"Oh! Yes, I did." Morgan held up a dress that had been lying over her arm. "The seamstresses just finished this. What do you think?"

Kim tilted her head back. "Looks okay," she said after a few seconds of scrutiny. "Very nice, actually."

"Very nice! Kim, it's breathtaking!" Nancy marveled. "I wish I could afford your clothes."

The outfit Morgan was holding was truly gorgeous and much less far-out than Kim's usual designs. It was a pearl-colored suit of watered silk, with a cropped jacket and slim knee-length skirt. A black, lacy camisole top peeked out from inside the jacket.

Kim smiled—a natural, unforced smile that made her seem a lot nicer. "This one's for me. I'm going to wear it to my opening. Hey, you look about my size," she said. "Would you like to try it on?"

"I'd love to."

"I'd like to see it on a model. You can change behind that screen in the corner. Morgan, Nancy and I are going to lunch in a second. Will you phone the restaurant downstairs to let them know we're coming?"

As Nancy stepped behind the screen, Kim called out, "I also designed the ruby pin on the jacket."

Nancy took a closer look at the pin. Its deep red stone was set in a simple silver frame. "It's beautiful! Is it real?" she called back.

"Of course not," answered Kim. "But you'd never know, would you?"

"*I* wouldn't." Nancy stepped into the skirt and pulled it up around her hips. It fit perfectly, just as Kim had predicted. She slipped the camisole and jacket on, marveling at the lustrous feel of the silk against her skin. The clasp on the pin hadn't been secured, and it pricked her a little, but fortunately it didn't draw blood. Nancy closed the clasp carefully and stepped out from behind the screen.

"Hey, it looks great on you!" exclaimed Kim. "And *you* look great in *it*. I may have to let you wear it in next week's show!"

Nancy turned to face the full-length mirror behind her. Kim was right—the outfit was incredibly flattering. It made her look totally sophisticated. "Now I know what 'looking like a million bucks' actually feels like," she said. "I'll just have to get one of these someday."

"Well, until then, how'd you like to wear it to lunch?" suggested Kim.

"You're sure? But what if I spill soup on it or something?"

"You won't," answered Kim. "And believe me, it'll be good publicity for me if you wear it. Just make sure you tell anyone who asks that *I* designed it!"

On their way to the restaurant they passed the manager's office as Bess and Sarah were leaving. Bess gasped out loud when she saw Nancy.

"You look great! I'd kill for that outfit!"

"Don't get too carried away," said Nancy, smiling. "How are you, Sarah?"

"Fine," muttered Sarah, gently touching the bandage under her eye. "I'd better get upstairs," she added, glancing at Kim. "Thanks a lot, Bess." She hurried away.

"Bess, you might as well come along with us,"

said Kim. "There's no sense in your hanging around upstairs—"

"Kim! I've been trying to reach you!"

Kim, Nancy, and Bess turned to see a handsome young man striding toward them, his dark eyes fixed on Kim's face.

"You've got more security than the president of the United States!" he said. "Your secretary won't put a call through to you. Your *sister* won't put a call through to you. And when I tried to get in to see you, I was stopped by a guard in a uniform. What's going on?"

Kim looked away. "It's just the security for my show," she said, her eyes averted. "I don't want my designs stolen. You know what it's like in this business."

"But you're not worried about *me!* Are you?" There was an eager expression in the man's eyes that made Nancy feel as though she should leave the two of them alone.

"If you two need to talk, Kim, Bess and I can meet you," she suggested.

"No! No! That's okay," Kim said quickly. Nancy wondered why she sounded so flustered. "Oh, I should introduce you," Kim went on. "This is Paul Lavalle. Paul, say hello to Bess Marvin and Nancy Drew."

"Hello to Bess Marvin and Nancy Drew," said Paul with a broad grin. "And hello to Kim Daley. By the way, what are you doing for lunch, Kim?"

"Having it with Nancy and Bess," Kim said

bluntly. "Nice to see you, Paul. Now I do have to be running along." She took both Bess and Nancy by the arm and led them toward the restaurant, moving so fast she was almost running.

Nancy cast a fleeting glance back at Paul, who was staring so hard at Kim that he didn't even notice Nancy. He looked hurt and confused—and angry. "Is Paul a friend of yours, Kim?" she asked in a low voice as they reached the restaurant's entrance.

"Not really. An old boyfriend, that's all," said Kim nonchalantly. "Kim Daley," she told the maître d'.

After they were seated, Bess looked around in awe. The restaurant certainly was beautiful. Potted palm trees were everywhere, filling the room with splashes of green. A miniature waterfall cascaded down one wall into a crystalline fish pond, and there were arrangements of brilliant tropical flowers on every table.

"Caesar salad for me," Kim told the waiter. "And a mineral water."

"I'll have a tossed salad," said Nancy. "For some reason I'm not very hungry. Bess, what are you having?"

"Oh, a salad, too, I guess," Bess said reluctantly. "No—wait. Make that, um, a turkey on a croissant and a side order of fries—and a chocolate shake. You only live once."

The minute the waiter had taken the menus

away, Kim's eyes began darting around the restaurant.

"Looks as though everyone I know is here today," she leaned in and told Nancy and Bess.

"Can you tell us about a few of them?" asked Nancy.

"Well, that's Apollo over there, having lunch with his agent. He's one of the city's top male models." Kim gestured toward a young man with intense dark eyes and a shock of long black hair. He was listening with a patient expression to a middle-aged woman sitting with him. "And over there's the fashion writer from the *Times*. She always wears the newest Japanese stuff." The editor was dressed in a gray coatdress as shapeless as a paper bag. "And there are Oscar Davis and Louella Teasdale from *Fashion*." Kim gestured toward another corner table, where Louella and Oscar were picking at their food.

"Those two would *love* to see me fall on my face," Kim continued.

"Why?" asked Nancy suspiciously.

"It makes better copy for the magazine, I guess," Kim said bitterly. "And take a peek at the table in the middle of the room. See that woman with the spiked hair?"

"How could anyone miss her?" asked Bess.

It wasn't only the spiked hair. The woman was dressed in a tight leather suit that had been dyed traffic-light yellow, and she was wearing ankle-high boots to match. She had on too much makeup, and her laugh rose raucously above all the other noise in the restaurant.

"That's Lina Roccocini, the designer," said Kim. "She always sits where everyone will see her. She's got a suite here in the hotel, too, the little copycat. Oops, she's seen me. Hi, darling!" Kim called to Lina, waving her napkin.

Lina waved back just as effusively. "Hello, sweetheart!" she called. Both women were obviously pretending there was no rivalry between them.

With an effort Nancy took her eyes off Lina. I must be hungry, she told herself. That's why it's so hard to concentrate. She took a drink of ice water, hoping to wake herself up.

"Kim," she said, "with your permission I'd like to call the police right after lunch. We should have them analyze whatever made that paperweight explode."

"No way!" said Kim emphatically. "Once the police know, there's no way to keep this thing quiet. And I don't want *any* negative publicity before this show!"

"But your life is in danger!" Nancy protested. "Don't you want to—"

She broke off as the waiter reached their table. With a flourish he placed a beautifully composed plate of greens in front of her. "Thanks," Nancy told him. "It looks great."

But what she was actually thinking was that she had no appetite at all. I wonder if I'm coming down with something, she thought as she reluctantly picked up her fork. The fork seemed so heavy!

Now, what had they been talking about before the food had come? Nancy tried to remember. Something about Kim . . . her show . . .

Nancy's head was starting to ache.

"Aren't you hungry, Nan?" asked Bess between bites of her sandwich.

"Uh—sure," Nancy said slowly. "It's just that it's so cold in here!" Shivering, she rubbed her arms to warm them. "And what's that ringing sound?"

Now both Kim and Bess were staring at her in alarm. "I don't hear any ringing," said Kim. "Are you okay, Nancy?"

"I'll be fine if you make them stop that ringing!" Nancy gasped. "It's hurting my head!"

She was racked with chills now. And the persistent ringing in her ears was growing louder and louder—unbearably loud.

Nancy stood up and took one step before she moaned once and crumpled to the floor. Darkness closed in on her.

Chapter

Three

A FOOT ABOVE NANCY, a face floated in midair. Nancy blinked, and the face became Bess's.

Bess's wide blue eyes were terrified. "Oh, thank heavens you're awake!" she gasped. "I was so worried! Someone's gone to call an ambulance."

"I don't need one," Nancy gasped, struggling to sit up. As she did, she noticed the ring of worried-looking people hovering behind Bess. "I must have some kind of virus. But I don't need to go to the hospital. If someone could just help me up to my room—"

"Well, we can do that, if it's what you really

want," said Bess. "But I hate to let this go without calling a doctor, Nan. Sure you're okay?"

Nancy *wasn't* sure. Her head still felt as if it were about to split open, and she was very shaky. But at least the horrible ringing sound seemed to have subsided. "I'll be fine once I get a nap," she said, forcing herself to smile.

I hope so, anyway, she added to herself.

Nancy didn't quite know how she got back to her room. She had only a vague memory of being supported by Kim and Bess. In fact, she didn't remember anything until the sound of the telephone jarred her awake.

Groping on the bedside table for the phone, she finally managed to find the receiver.

She cleared her throat. "Hello?" she murmured.

"Nancy? You sound so far away. Did I wake you?" It was Ned.

"Kind of," Nancy said. "Hang on a sec. Let me find the light switch."

"What's going on?" asked Ned. "Are you asleep? It's not dark yet!"

Nancy rolled out of bed and stumbled toward the window. She patted the wall until she found the curtain pull, then gave the cord a yank. Fading November sunshine filtered into the room.

Nancy climbed back onto the bed. "There,

that's better," she said. "Anyway, what I'm doing here is sleeping off some sort of virus that kind of attacked me at lunch."

Ned laughed. "So you're not Superwoman after all. Or maybe you just need Superman to fly to your side?"

Nancy laughed, too. "Could be. It's been quite a day." Quickly she filled him in on what had happened since she and Bess had arrived.

"Sounds pretty exciting," Ned said when she'd finished. "Wish I were there."

"Oh, I wish you were, too, Ned. *That* would drive this bug away for sure."

Just then the door to her room was slowly pushed in, and a head of fluffy blond hair poked around it. "Nan, you awake? It's me— Bess."

Nancy nodded and smiled. "Ned, I have to go. I'll check in with you as soon as I can. I love you," she said in a lower voice.

"I love you, too," said Ned. "Take care of yourself, Nancy."

Nancy hung up and looked at her watch. It was almost five o'clock. "I can't believe I've been out for four hours!" she said to Bess.

"You were out the second you hit the bed. Are you feeling better?"

"Much better. I'm going to stay down while we talk, though." Nancy punched her pillow up against the headboard and lay back against it.

"Now—tell me everything that happened after you brought me here," she ordered.

Bess perched herself on the edge of the bed. "Well, Kim and I went back downstairs and had our lunches. Mine was great . . . you didn't mean *every* detail, did you." Bess grinned at herself. "Anyway, that guy Paul Lavalle came in and joined Lina, but then he excused himself and wandered over to our table to talk.

"You know I have very high standards, and that Paul Lavalle is a major hunk. But, sigh, I think he still likes Kim, even though *she* says it's all over. And I also think that Lina likes *him*. While he was talking to us, I kept looking over at Lina. She looked really, really mad. Later Kim told me Paul's a fabulous photographer," Bess went on. "She also said that if things weren't so awkward between them, she'd love to have Paul working for her again. So, how'd I do, Ms. Detective?"

"Great," Nancy said, already absorbed in her thoughts. "I don't see why Paul would threaten Kim—not if he still likes her."

Nancy pushed herself up and slowly began to pace the room. "I'd like to know more about Lina Roccocini," she added.

"She's got motive, for sure," said Bess, joining Nancy's musings.

"But she's almost *too* obvious. I mean, Lina is

successful—so would she jeopardize her success by attempting to blow up the competition?"

"I guess you're right," Bess said. "It has to be someone pretty desperate."

There was a soft rap on the door. "It's open," called Nancy. "Come on in!"

The door swung in silently, and Morgan Daley stopped on the threshold. "Uh, hi," she said nervously. "I hope I'm not disturbing you, but Kim sent me to see if I could, well, do anything to help."

"That's nice," said Nancy. "I really am fine. Could I ask you a few questions, though?" Morgan nodded. "Won't you sit down?" Nancy gestured toward an armchair.

Morgan sat on the edge of the chair and remained awkwardly silent. "Could you tell me a little about what you do?" Nancy asked. "You work mainly for Kim, right?" Morgan nodded. "Do you like it?"

"Pretty much," said Morgan. "I mean, she's so talented that it's really a privilege just to help her. And talented people—well, of course they're sort of difficult at times, but I'm sure she doesn't mean to be. Difficult, I mean." She broke off, blushing.

"What kinds of things do you do for her?" Nancy asked.

"Oh, a little of everything. Answer the phone, run errands, make lunch reservations, pay the bills, pick up fabric books—stuff like that. You know."

Nancy didn't know exactly, but she was starting to get the idea. Kim handled all the fun parts of her business, and Morgan cleaned up all the messes. "You don't help with the creative work?" Nancy asked, just to make sure.

"Oh, no. Kim doesn't need that kind of help," Morgan said. "I just handle the day-to-day stuff. It's kind of fun, actually."

Hmmm, Nancy thought. Morgan sounded too good to be true. Could she actually enjoy all the drudgery? Was it possible that she had a secret grudge against Kim?

"I really have to be getting back upstairs," Morgan said suddenly. "Sarah's taking the afternoon off, so I'm doing double work. If you don't need me anymore—"

Just then someone rapped sharply on the door, which flew open before Nancy could respond. Kim stormed in, waving a newspaper. "First the calls," she said furiously. "Then the explosion. And now *this!*"

She yanked the paper open and shoved it into Nancy's face. A column had been circled in black. The caption was *"Entre nous,"* and the author was Louella Teasdale.

"If you're not familiar with this trash," said Kim, "it's about time you got acquainted with the dirtiest gossip column in the Midwest. *Entre nous* is French for 'just between us.' All the garbage fit to print by the biggest garbage collector of them all."

She began reading in a voice that was staccato with rage.

"'What famous—or, should I say, infamous—high-fashion teen designer with the initials K.D. has been on the receiving end of nasty phone calls? Yes, it's true. The as-yet unidentified caller may be a disgruntled customer—but who'd make death threats just because a design was bad? Far more likely that the glamorous K.D. has been lording it over too many people. She certainly has the reputation for treating some folks pretty shabbily. The high point of this sudsy soap opera came today when somebody exploded a crystal paperweight in K.D.'s office. My advice to K.D. is: Don't look into any more crystal balls. You just may have seen the future—and it's *b-a-d.*'" Kim snapped the paper shut and threw it down on the bed.

"I didn't do it!" Morgan said, even though no one had even looked at her. "Louella tried to pump me for news, but I never said a word. She didn't get a thing out of me, I promise!"

"No one's accusing you, Morgan," said Nancy.

Morgan continued as if she hadn't heard. "And I never even spoke to Oscar. I don't know who could have told them. I'm sure it wasn't any of the models, and I can't believe it was Sarah, either."

Kim had been looking angrier and angrier as Morgan spoke, and now she exploded. "Morgan, shut up!" She picked up the paper and rammed it into the wastebasket. "I'm going to ruin whoever leaked this!"

Abruptly she broke off and stared at her sister.

"Morgan, what are you wearing?" she asked.

"Just—just an old sweater," replied Morgan, edging back into her chair.

"Not the old sweater!" snapped Kim. "The new jewelry!"

Nancy followed Kim's gaze. Half hidden under Morgan's collar was a silver-and-ruby pin exactly like the one Nancy had worn earlier. Nancy didn't know why she hadn't noticed it before.

"That's a copy of my design," Kim said menacingly. "Where did you get it?"

Morgan stood up and backed away toward the door. Her body was stiff.

"I—I found it in a secondhand shop during my lunch break today," she stammered. "It's—it's just a coincidence, Kim—"

The words were barely out of her mouth before Kim leaped forward and ripped the pin off Morgan's sweater—unraveling the gray wool into long strings.

"I bet you copied my design," she said, throwing the pin to the ground. Her face was pale with rage. "I *know* that's what you did. That's what you've always done—copy everything about me."

And before Nancy could stop her, Kim slapped Morgan—hard—across the cheek.

"You'll pay for this, Morgan," she said in a flat, dead voice. "I'll make sure you do." And she turned and strode out of the room.

Chapter

Four

MORGAN STOOD STARING, openmouthed, at the door her sister had just slammed. Then she took a deep breath—and burst into tears.

"The pin doesn't mean a thing!" she wailed. "I *didn't* copy it! It's nothing like Kim's pin, anyway —look for yourself! The design around the stone is completely different!" She picked the pin up from the carpet and held it out to Nancy and Bess.

As far as Nancy could tell, Morgan's pin was exactly like the one on the outfit Kim had designed. "It doesn't look so different to me," Nancy said diplomatically after a second. "But I didn't really get much of a chance to look at the other pin."

"Well, they're really nothing at all the same," said Morgan with a touch of defiance in her voice, "but I don't suppose Kim will believe I wasn't trying to copy her." She pulled a tissue out of her purse and blew her nose. "I'd better be getting back upstairs," she said.

"Would you like a soda or something before you go up?" Nancy asked. Morgan's face was so tearstained and splotchy that she wanted to give her time to compose herself. "I could call room service."

Morgan shook her head. "Kim won't want me to be late. Thanks, though. Maybe another time." She sounded wistful.

"Whew!" Bess whistled after Morgan had left. "Speaking of soap operas, *that* was a lovely little scene. Poor Morgan!"

"I feel sorry for her, too," said Nancy. "I mean, Kim definitely overreacted—but how can Morgan keep saying the pins are different? I *wouldn't* be able to tell them apart if I saw them together. I think something more is going on here than just Kim's being mean to Morgan. But I have no idea what it is."

Nancy was feeling better after a snack and was eager to get more information. She and Bess took the elevator down to the newspaper stand in the lobby and bought every paper to find out who else might be printing gossip about Kim Daley.

Everyone, it seemed. Each fashion columnist had something to say about the calls and the explosion. But none was more vindictive than Bronwen Weiss at the Chicago *Tattler*.

As Nancy read the *Tattler* column, Bess peered over her shoulder and shook her head. "This one is horrible!" she said. "I never heard of Bronwen Weiss. Who is she?"

"I've never heard of her, either," answered Nancy. "She must be new."

"Someone has it in for Kim Daley, our town's would-be trendy designer of exclusive teen wear," the column began. "After a series of threatening phone calls, a possibly incendiary device was planted in Daley's office. Things were such a mess in there that the police could find no sign of the device this afternoon. The police only learned of the explosion after this reporter called to confirm the bomb rumor.

"The message is clear, though—Kim Daley, get out of the business before it's too late. The only question I have is why did it take this mystery person so long to do what so many have *wanted* to do since Kim Daley became a star?"

Bess shuddered. "Boy, I hope I never get on Bronwen Weiss's bad side. I wonder who leaked this story to the press," she added thoughtfully.

"If we knew that, the whole mystery would probably be solved," Nancy said. "Other than you, me, Kim, Sarah, and Morgan, who else had access to the office?" Nancy sighed. "Everyone on the staff, of course. It's beyond me."

"Of course it *could* all be a publicity stunt. That's what one of these papers hints at—" Bess began.

"No," Nancy answered decisively, setting the stack of papers on the newsstand. "It's more than that, I'm sure. What do you say? Let's get out there and start talking to suspects. And I suggest we start with Lina Roccocini."

"Okay," said Bess agreeably. "Sometimes the obvious suspect is the real villain after all."

Nancy laughed. "Is that something you read in a fortune cookie?"

"Hey, don't knock fortune cookies!" Bess protested. "I had one last week that said I'd meet the love of my life before the year is out."

"Six weeks to go," said Nancy. "Good luck."

At the information desk in the lobby, they were given the number of Lina's suite, which turned out to be on the twenty-ninth floor, directly below Kim's. They took the elevator up, and Nancy rapped hard at the door.

No answer—just coughing and the scurrying of footsteps from the other side of the door. Nancy knocked again, and finally a voice called out, "Just a minute."

A *long* minute later the door opened, and a plump, round-faced young blond woman peered out at them owlishly from behind huge glasses.

"May I help you?" she asked.

"My name is Nancy Drew, and this is my associate, Bess Marvin. We'd like to speak with Lina Roccocini, please."

"She's—uh—she's not really available right now," the young woman said. "It's after hours, you know. Do you have an appointment?"

"No," answered Nancy, "but it is important. Perhaps I could leave her a message?"

"Oh, okay," said the woman. "Come on in. You may use the desk." As she waved them inside, Nancy noticed that she had a small birthmark—a pinkish spot—just above her left eyebrow.

"I'm Alison Haber, Lina's assistant," the woman told them as Nancy sat down at the desk. "Sorry I can't be more helpful, but we're kind of busy getting ready for the show."

"I understand," said Nancy. Quickly she jotted down a few words on a sheet of hotel stationery. "But it's very important that I talk to her. Here's my room and phone number. If you could tell her to call me as soon as possible—"

Just then a side door in the suite flew open, and Paul Lavalle came barreling out with his arms full of photographs mounted on white cardboard frames.

"These are all ready to go to the printer, Alison," he began. Then he caught sight of Nancy and Bess—and gave a start. "Hi! We meet again!" he said with a tense smile. "How are you?"

The stack of pictures started to slip out of his arms. "Here, Paul! Let me take those!" said Alison, dashing forward. As Paul handed her the pictures, Alison gazed up at him with such adoration that Nancy was startled. This girl is head over heels in love! she said to herself.

Paul didn't seem to notice Alison. He was still staring at Nancy. "Are you wondering what Kim's old boyfriend—well, not that old—is doing hanging out with her archrival?" he asked.

"Not really," said Nancy mildly. "What you do is your own business. I guess it's a little bit strange that you're here with Kim's competition, but—"

"Let me explain, then," said Paul bitingly. "I'm a free-lance photographer. And I'm good. I made Kim look good. I mean, the way I lit her creations—the way I positioned her models—I think a good deal of her early success was due to me.

"Then she dumped me. Which hurt a lot. Kim and I had a really great relationship, both business-wise and—social-wise. . . ." His voice trailed off, and Bess glanced uncomfortably at Nancy.

"You don't have to go into details, Paul!" Alison blurted out. "These girls are strangers!"

"I'm not going into details," Paul said, his eyes

still on Nancy. "Anyway, *I* was very happy with our arrangement—but Kim thought I was trying to dominate her life." He turned away and stared out the window. "From her point of view, falling in love meant losing control. So she dumped me."

"Her loss," said Alison, and turned beet red.

Again Paul paid no attention to Alison. "Well," he said with a sigh, "a guy's got to make a living. So I signed on with Lina. And we're both delighted with the arrangement," he added more cheerfully. "Lina really cares about what I think, unlike Kim. I couldn't be happier."

Nancy wasn't sure how true that was, but she didn't say anything. She was wondering whether Lina was in this suite or not. *Someone* was certainly walking around behind the door of the inner office—she could hear quick footsteps pacing back and forth. Was it Lina? And were these two protecting her? Or was she afraid to come out?

Alison's voice broke into Nancy's thoughts. "You look tired, Paul," she said gently. "Can I get you something? A mineral water? Juice?" She looked so lovesick that Nancy almost felt embarrassed for her.

"No thanks, honey," said Paul with genuine kindness in his voice. "That's nice of you, though." Alison's eyes lit up, and again she blushed dark red.

But her face fell at Paul's next words. "You

looked great in that dress of Kim's, Nancy," he said. "You know, you really should think about modeling some of Lina's clothes. They'd look fabulous on you. Here, let me show you a few of her designs."

"No!" Alison cried out. "No one's allowed to see the designs—not before the show!"

Paul gently put a hand on Alison's shoulder, and she flinched as if she'd been burned.

"These girls aren't spies, Alison," he said. "Don't worry. It can't do any harm."

"Lina's going to be mad," Alison said nervously.

"There's nothing for her to be mad *about*. Nancy's not out to get her! Now, why don't you be a good girl and run those pix out to the printer's? They're keeping the shop open late for us."

For a second it looked as though Alison was going to say something more. Then she sighed and picked up the stack of photographs. "Okay, Paul," she said quietly, and left the suite.

Paul grinned. "She's nice, but she tends to take life a little too seriously. Here—let me get those sketches."

As he went out, Nancy took a quick glance around the room and was surprised. One corner was filled with electronics equipment— microphones, an elaborate tape deck, and lots of recording equipment.

Nancy strolled over to get a closer look. What?

she thought. One of the pieces of equipment was a voice-distortion apparatus. She'd seen one just like it on a TV show about how special effects were produced. And here, in this makeshift fashion studio, was a similar voice-changing machine. What possible use could Lina have for this electronic equipment? Unless . . .

"Excuse me, Paul," Nancy began, "but what do you use this vocoder for?"

Just as she reached over to inspect it more closely, Paul grabbed her by the elbow and violently yanked her away. "Hey, don't touch! That's expensive stuff!" he said.

"She wasn't touching anything!" Bess said indignantly.

"She's right, Paul," Nancy said, rubbing her arm. "I just wanted to look."

"I'm really sorry if I overreacted," said Paul sheepishly, "but that's very delicate equipment. If anything were to happen to it, Lina would take it out of my paycheck. I'm sure you can understand."

He glanced at his watch. "Look," he added suddenly, "would it be okay if I showed you those sketches another time? I've really got to get back to work. I'll tell Lina you came by, and I'm sure she'll call you. Can you let yourselves out?"

As he talked, his eyes kept straying to the vocoder. And Nancy had the feeling she knew why.

"Of course, Paul," she said smoothly. "We understand. Thanks for your help."

"*What* help?" Bess snorted once they were safely out in the hotel corridor again. "All he did was blab about Kim and kick us out. And I was really beginning to like the guy, too! So much for my taste in men. And so much for fortune cookies!"

"Oh, he helped more than he knew," Nancy said. "I'm sure that that's the vocoder that's being used to distort the voices on those calls to Kim. And Paul didn't want me to know anything about it. That means . . ."

"He made those calls?" Beth asked.

"Maybe. Or maybe he knows some other reason why the vocoder shouldn't be seen. Either way he gave himself away in there.

"What time is it, anyway?" she asked. "I left my watch back in our room."

Bess checked her watch. "Six-thirty. Dinnertime?" she asked hopefully.

Nancy chuckled. "Getting there, anyway. I'd just like to go up to Kim's suite first and see if she's there. Let's take the stairs—just one floor."

At the top of the flight, Nancy paused. "I've got to catch my breath," she panted. "Those steps are steeper than I thought." She sighed in exasperation. "I guess whatever I caught hasn't gone away yet."

"Nan, are you sure you're okay?" Bess asked in

a worried voice. "It's not like you to get shaky from a few stairs!"

"I'm fine now," Nancy said after a second. She opened the door to Kim's floor. "Let's go and—"

At that moment a terrible scream echoed up and down the corridor. A bone-chilling shriek of pure terror that increased in volume as the seconds passed.

"Oh, no! She's dying!" The wail changed from one note to words.

Nancy raced down the corridor as fast as she could. "Hurry, Bess," she gasped. "It's coming from Kim's suite—something terrible must have happened!"

Chapter

Five

"HELP! SOMEONE PLEASE *help!*" The cries for help grew more and more panicky as Nancy and Bess approached the open door to Kim's suite.

The guard was gone—he had joined a small cluster of frightened-looking people standing just outside the entrance to Kim's office. Kim was inside the office—screaming.

Nancy and Bess pushed their way into the office. They stopped short.

Kim was kneeling on the floor next to her dog. The dog was lying motionless, her back arched stiffly and her legs straight out in front of her. Her

45

sides were heaving, and her brown eyes were filled with fear as they looked beseechingly up at Kim.

"Chanel! Chanel! Oh, what's happened to her?" Kim was in tears.

She saw Nancy and scrambled to her feet. "Thank goodness you're here! I think Chanel's had a stroke or something! Where's Morgan? Has she called the animal hospital? Why do I have to do everything myself?"

A breathless Morgan appeared at the door. "They're on their way," she said, and stepped back outside.

"Oh, please, let them get here soon!" Kim moaned.

Nancy put a soothing hand on Kim's shoulder. "I'm sure they're coming as fast as they can. Now, why don't you tell me what happened while we wait?"

"I don't really *know* what happened!" Kim said. "I was making a cup of tea. When Chanel saw me stirring it, she came running up for a taste. She loves tea." Kim's eyes filled with tears. "So I gave her a little bit in her dish. Then the phone rang. When I hung up, the tea was gone— and Chanel was like this." She gestured toward the floor.

"Did you drink any of the tea?" Nancy asked immediately.

"No. I didn't have a chance. I accidentally knocked over the cup and broke it when I answered the phone." Her expression changed. "Do you think Chanel's been poisoned?"

"It looks as though she might have been," said Nancy.

"You mean if I'd drunk that tea, I might have been poisoned too?"

"Yes—*if* it was poisoned. Let's wait and see. Where are the pieces of the cup?"

"Uh, I don't know," said Kim, momentarily distracted from her grief. "I broke it when I answered the phone, and someone must have cleaned it up while I was talking." She looked into her wastebasket. "But, wait, this has been emptied! Morgan!" she yelled. "Where's my trash?"

Again Morgan appeared at the door. "I dumped it down the trash chute," she said. "Why? Was that the wrong thing to do?"

"You picked this time to get fastidious," Kim screeched. "Do you realize that now we have no way to check whether there was poison in that tea?"

"Oh, no!" Two bright spots of color appeared high on Morgan's cheeks. "I'm so sorry," she whispered. "I just wanted to be helpful."

"Forget it," Kim snapped. "It's too late now."

"The animal ambulance is here," someone said as a young man raced into the room. Quickly Kim told him what had happened.

"I'll get her to the hospital right away so they can find out what's wrong," he said.

The young man scooped up the stiff dog and headed out the front door, and all the workers went back to their jobs or to their homes.

Kim flung herself down at her desk and buried her face in her hands. "I just know she's not going to make it," she cried. She looked up at Nancy, her face suddenly savage. "You *really* have to find whoever's been doing this."

"I will," Nancy promised. I've got to, she added to herself. How long will it be before this person tries to hurt Kim again?

"There's not much I can do tonight, though, Kim," Nancy added. "It's already after seven. Can't you take a break?"

Kim wearily rubbed a hand across her eyes. "No," she said dully. "We have to keep working. For the next few days we're going to be totally swamped. At least it'll keep my mind off Chanel—I hope."

"Then if there's nothing I can do for you tonight, I think I'll go back to our suite." And collapse, Nancy added to herself. Must be that virus acting up again, she thought. Well, a good night's sleep would take care of it.

But just as she and Bess reached the door, Lina Roccocini pushed in past them. So she had been in her suite all the time, just as Nancy had suspected! Paul and Alison were right behind her.

"Who on *earth* was making all that noise?" Lina demanded imperiously. "Don't you know some of us have work to do? It's impossible to concentrate with all the yammering in here! Really, Kim, you should try to keep your staff under control."

Kim looked as if she were about to explode. But with a visible effort she swallowed whatever she'd been about to say. "I'm afraid I was the one doing the 'yammering,' darling," she told Lina in a silky voice. "So sorry to disturb you. We had a bit of an emergency here, but it's all taken care of now. And has been for the past ten minutes," she added, letting Lina know that she had taken a long time going up one flight of stairs.

"Another emergency?" Lina asked. "What happened this time? Another bomb?"

"We think her dog's been poisoned!" Morgan burst out.

Lina looked a little ashamed of herself. "Your dog? I'm so sorry to hear it," she said awkwardly. Then she seemed to recover herself. "Well, see you around," she continued. "Come on, Paul— Alison. Maybe we'll be able to get something done now that all the noise is over."

She walked out, followed by Alison and a sheepish-looking Paul.

Nancy nodded to Bess, and they followed Lina out the door. Nancy stayed as close to Lina as she could, hoping she might overhear something— and she did.

"If you ask me, they poisoned the wrong animal," Lina was muttering.

"That's a horrible thing to say!" Paul burst out.

"It's disgusting the way Kim would use any gimmick to get attention. I wish she'd just die and leave the rest of the fashion world in peace!"

Paul stopped short. "What are you saying, Lina?" he asked, astounded. "You don't sound like yourself. I know you're a prima donna, but you're taking it a bit far, don't you think?"

Lina looked as though Paul had hit her. "I didn't mean it! Really, I didn't!" she exclaimed. "You're right, Paul. I went overboard. She just really, really gets on my nerves." She took his hand. "Thanks for blowing the whistle."

"Let's just forget about it," Paul muttered, pulling free and turning toward the stairs. "I overreacted, too. It's just that— Well, as I said, let's just forget about it."

Alison had been completely silent during this exchange. She'd just been drifting along next to Paul. Now, for the first time, she spoke.

"I—I think I'll take a walk," she said.

"A walk? But it's dark—and it's freezing out there!" Lina exclaimed.

Alison didn't meet her boss's eye. "I'll be all right," she said. "I won't take long. I just—just need to get some air."

Nancy wondered if what was really bothering Alison was the fact that Paul had defended Kim so ardently. It was kind of sad, she thought, that no one seemed to pay any attention to Alison. Like Morgan, Alison was completely overshadowed by her boss.

"I'll see you later," Alison said in a choked voice, and she hurried down the hall toward the elevators.

"I wonder if she's all right—" Just then Lina noticed Nancy for the first time. "Oh, hi!" she exclaimed. "I didn't see you! You're the ones who were having lunch with Kim today, aren't you?"

Then her voice sharpened. "Why are you following me?"

"We just left at the same time you did," Nancy said evenly. "But I *am* investigating these threats and attempts to kill Kim. I left a message in your suite—"

"Oh, that was you?" Lina interrupted. "Well, I'd be happy to talk to you, but I've got to get back to work tonight. Tomorrow would work a little better for me. Would that be okay?

"Would that be okay?" Lina repeated.

Nancy didn't answer. She had just noticed the pin on Lina's scarf.

A silver pin with a ruby at its center. A pin just like the one Morgan Daley had been wearing— and just like the one-of-a-kind pin Kim had designed. Where had Lina gotten it? Nancy met Lina's eyes.

"What's the matter?" Lina asked.

"Nothing," Nancy said. How could I have been so obvious? she wondered. I must be even more tired than I thought!

Lina was looking wary now. "You're not a spy, are you?" she asked with an attempt at a laugh.

"Did Kim send you, or are you working for some other designer?"

"I promise you we're nothing of the—"

"Oh, sure," Lina interrupted. "Is that why you just happened to turn up before the show?"

Suddenly she turned and bolted through the stairwell door.

"Lina! Where are you going?" Paul called down after her.

"To call security!" Lina shot back. "I want these two girls thrown out of the hotel!"

Chapter

Six

"THERE'S NO NEED to throw us out of here," Nancy said as calmly as she could. Lina halted on the landing and looked doubtfully up at her. "Bess and I are definitely not spies," Nancy went on, "and I'm sorry if I gave you that impression. I was just looking at the pin you were wearing and wondering where you got it."

"What pin?" Lina asked.

"The silver one on your scarf . . ." Nancy blinked. There was no pin on Lina's scarf now. "Did you take it off?" she asked Lina.

"I haven't taken anything off," Lina said. "Would somebody please explain what's going on here?"

"You were wearing a silver pin with a ruby in the center," Nancy told her. "It was just like one Kim Daley had designed."

Now Lina was staring at Nancy. "Are you all right?" she asked. "You really don't look well, you know. And I definitely don't know what you're talking about."

"But—" Nancy stopped. Her thoughts were whirling. Lina had to have been wearing the pin—otherwise, why had she thought Nancy was a spy when she caught her looking at it? But what if there really hadn't been a pin on Lina's scarf? What if Nancy had just imagined it?

Chills began to creep up Nancy's spine again, and all of a sudden she felt much too exhausted to think about anything except bed.

"I'm sorry," she said, leaning against the wall. "I must have made a mistake. Did *you* see a pin on Lina's scarf, Bess?"

"I—I wasn't looking for one." Bess faltered. "I didn't notice, Nan."

"Neither did I," said Paul.

"Okay," Nancy said tiredly. "As I said, Lina, I'm sorry. It's been a long day—maybe we can talk tomorrow. Let's go, Bess."

Nancy collapsed onto her bed the minute they got back to their suite. "Ooooh," she moaned. "Did I just make a fool of myself or what?"

"You never make a fool of yourself," said Bess,

sitting down on the edge of the bed. "But what exactly was that all about?"

"I could have sworn Lina was wearing another copy of that silver-and-ruby pin Kim designed," said Nancy. "You know, like the one Kim yelled at Morgan for wearing. I'm sure she took it off on the stairs after she'd noticed me looking at it. But I'm not *positive*. I guess I could have imagined it—only I never do things like that, do I?"

"Never," Bess told her. "Of course, you *have* been sick . . ."

"I know I have. But I'm not delirious." Nancy's voice was more confident now. "She must have slipped the pin off. And that means there's definitely a connection between Lina and Morgan. But what?"

"Well, whatever it is, it'll keep till tomorrow," Bess said. "You should get some food and rest, Nan. Stop thinking about the case and concentrate on dinner instead. I'm starving, and you should be, too. You know what they say— feed a cold, starve a fever, feed a virus." She grinned. "Or at least *I* think that's what they say."

"I'm really not hungry," Nancy said. "Go ahead and order something for yourself, Bess, and get me a glass of milk. I'll drink it in the bathtub. I'm freezing. I want to take a nice, hot bath for about ten hours."

Forty-five minutes later Nancy crawled into

bed. "Now, are you sure you're okay?" Bess fretted, tucking an extra blanket around her friend.

"I'll be fine tomorrow," Nancy said. "Thanks, Bess."

Boy, she thought drowsily as she pulled the covers up under her chin, the fashion world is a real-life soap opera. Paul loves Kim. Lina loves Paul. *Alison* loves Paul. Kim hates Paul. Lina hates Kim—and who knows how many other people hate Kim, too? Morgan? Sarah? Every gossip columnist in Chicago? All those people— and any one of them could be a murderer!

Well, Bess was right—there was no use thinking about it now. Nancy snuggled down into her pillow and fell asleep. . . .

She was walking down a models' runway dressed in a floor-length black velvet dress. It was swelteringly hot. No one had told her what to do, and she wasn't quite sure she'd put the dress on right. As she walked down the runway, she suddenly heard people scream. Startled, Nancy glanced into the audience, where Bess and Ned were watching her with absolute horror on their faces. What was wrong?

Suddenly Kim rushed out from behind a curtain. "The pin! You forgot the pin!" she shrieked at Nancy. "The outfit won't *work* without it!" She pinned a huge silver-and-ruby brooch onto Nancy's dress, but it was so heavy that it pulled Nancy forward. She was falling . . . falling. . . .

Nancy sat up in bed, sweat pouring off her face, her heart pounding. She pushed off all the covers, but it didn't help. Frantically she rushed into the bathroom and splashed cold water on her face.

"Nan?" She heard Bess call sleepily. "Are you all right?"

"I'm fine," Nancy said. "Just hot, that's all. Sorry I woke you."

Now her teeth were chattering. This water is too cold! she thought fretfully. She groped her way back to bed, where she slipped under all available covers. Then she curled up into a ball. Shivering, she waited for the bed to warm up. It was a long, long time before she fell asleep again.

When she woke up, Bess was standing beside the bed, dressed in an oversize yellow sweater, denim jacket, and jeans.

"You were sleeping so soundly I didn't have the heart to wake you," Bess said. "Want some breakfast?"

"Give me half an hour," said Nancy with a yawn. "I'll meet you in the lobby."

When Bess had left, Nancy stumbled to the shower. How can I still feel so tired? she asked herself as she stepped into the steaming water. Even lifting the soap seemed like more trouble than it was worth, and getting dressed was worse yet. When she'd finished brushing her hair, Nancy felt ready for a nap.

As she was leaving she noticed a piece of paper lying on the floor just in front of the door.

Nancy picked up the thick paper, which had been folded over once. Her name had been typed on it with some kind of electronic printer.

Slowly Nancy lifted the top half and began reading.

Dear Nancy Drew:

I'm sorry that I can't reveal my identity, but in a minute you'll understand why. My case is not against you. I'm sure you're a nice person. You just got in the way accidentally, and I'm really sorry. It's not really my fault, though. Blame Kim Daley, not me.

Blame Kim for what? wondered Nancy. Frowning, she read on.

Please take this *very* seriously and do what I tell you. Get to a hospital right away. The poison wasn't meant for you—

"Poison!" Nancy gasped.

but it's fatal. If you're not treated within seventy-two hours of the time you got the dose, you'll die!

Chapter

Seven

THE NOTE FELL from Nancy's hand and fluttered to the floor as she sat down on the edge of her bed. Her mind was reeling. Slowly she picked up the note and read the message again.

I'm sure you're a nice person. You just got in the way . . . If you're not treated within seventy-two hours of the time you got the dose, you'll die!

Nancy's hand was trembling so much that the words were a blur. "It can't be true," she whispered.

But it had to be true. Everything fell into place. The way Nancy had passed out at lunch the day before . . . her inexplicable tiredness . . . the flashes of intense heat and cold she'd been feeling . . . It all made a horrible kind of sense.

"I don't have a virus," Nancy said aloud. "I'm dying."

Panic was stifling her. If she didn't get control of herself, Nancy knew, she'd faint. She leaned forward, put her head between her knees, and forced herself to count to twenty very slowly. Then she stood up.

First things first, she thought to herself—and the first thing I want is to have Ned here. Nancy knew she'd never get through this crisis without him there to support her. She dialed his number quickly. And when he answered on the first ring, Nancy was utterly speechless.

"Hello? Hello?" Ned said. "Who's there?"

"Ned!" she said finally, trying to sound as normal as possible. "I'm glad you're home."

"Hi, Nan!" Ned said jubilantly. "Feeling better, I hope?"

"Well, not exactly," Nancy said. "Listen, Ned—"

"What's the matter?" he asked instantly.

"A lot. I hate to screw up your vacation, but I've got to have you here with me. I—I can't even ask you if it's okay." Nancy's voice was wobbling. She cleared her throat and went on. "I just have to have you here. Can you drive to Chicago right away? I promise to explain everything when you get here."

Ned didn't ask any questions. "I'll leave now" was all he said.

"Thank you," Nancy said. "I love you so much."

"I love you, too. I'll be there before you know it."

Now to call Hannah. Somehow Nancy had to *try* to get in touch with her father.

"Hannah, it's me," she said. "I was just wondering—did Dad leave a number?"

"Oh, no. Nothing at all. He said there was no number *to* leave. Why? Is there something wrong?"

Suddenly Nancy couldn't stand to tell her just how wrong everything was. If she couldn't get in touch with her father, she didn't want Hannah to know what was the matter, either. "Nothing important," she said casually. "I just wanted to see how he was doing."

"Don't try to pretend with me, Nancy Drew," said Hannah. "I know you too well. What's going on? Come on, out with it."

"It's nothing! Really!" said Nancy. "I just need to pick his brains on some legal stuff. Guess I'm out of luck, but if he should happen to call in, could you do me a favor and ask him to give me a ring? Okay?"

"Not okay," said Hannah. "Now you tell me what's going on. You sound terrible."

Nancy took a deep breath, trying to compose herself. "Must be this connection. I have to run, but please, please tell Dad to call me. Thanks. Love you. 'Bye!" She hung up before Hannah could say anything else.

Okay, that's out of the way, she said to herself. Now I have to leave a message for Bess.

She picked up a piece of hotel stationery and scribbled a note to attach to the note from the poisoner. "Don't panic," it said, "but after you read this, take it to the police for a fingerprint check. I'm going to the nearest hospital. Be back as soon as possible."

Then she paused. Her heart was fluttering in her chest like a wild thing trying to break free. She could barely catch her breath as she left the suite for the elevator.

Bess was waiting in the lobby, impatiently tapping her foot. Her face lit up when she saw Nancy.

"What took you so long? Listen, the cutest guy just went into the Oak Room. Let's eat in there so I can—"

"Bess, listen," Nancy interrupted. "I can't explain right now, but go up to our suite. I left a note for you. I'll try to get back as soon as I can." She hated to leave Bess without telling her what was going on, but she just didn't have the strength for an emotional public scene.

Bess was looking disappointed. "Can't you at least clue me in?"

"Nope," said Nancy tersely. "I have to go. Thanks, Bess."

As Bess headed for the elevator, Nancy approached the front desk. "Where's the nearest hospital?" she asked the day manager.

"There's a very good hospital at Sandburg Terrace. It's about a ten- or fifteen-minute drive."

Nancy raced out the front door and hailed a cab. "Hurry, please," she begged the driver. "It's an emergency."

"Okay, miss." The cab lurched forward, zoomed down the street, then slowed to a crawl —and stopped. "Uh-oh," the driver said with a chuckle. "I forgot. It's Celebrate Scandinavia Day." An endless parade strolled with maddening slowness down the street.

Nancy felt so tense she wanted to scream. She leaned forward in her seat.

"Driver, is there a side street? Is there another way to Sandburg Terrace?"

"Only if I make a U-turn, which wouldn't be too smart with that cop standing right there."

"I do see him," Nancy said. "But I've been poisoned, and I have to find a doctor. Please— make the turn."

The driver turned around in his seat and grinned sarcastically. "That's the first time I've ever heard *that* one," he said. "Pretty good, lady."

Nancy looked straight into his eyes. "Do I look as though I'm kidding?" she asked.

The cabbie's eyes widened. "No, you don't, now that you mention it. Okay, you got it."

He spun the steering wheel. The cab leaped into a sharp one-hundred-and-eighty-degree turn, swerving out of the path of a truck, whose driver let go with a stream of curses. The police officer blew his whistle angrily as the cab shot past a yellow warning sign, made a tire-screeching left turn, and headed toward Lakeshore Drive.

Nancy had been thrown back against the seat of the cab when it turned. "Don't get me killed before I get to the hospital," she panted, "but don't slow down, either. You're doing great."

Still, the five minutes it took to reach the hospital's emergency exit seemed agonizingly long. "Thank you, thank you," cried Nancy, jumping out of the cab before it had even come to a full stop. She thrust some money into the driver's hand through the window. "Keep the change," she said over her shoulder as she dashed away. "You earned it!"

She ran to the admissions desk and told her story to the sleepy-eyed woman sitting there.

"I'm afraid all our doctors are busy," the woman droned. "I really don't know when—"

"I don't have time to wait!" Nancy cried. "Please help me!"

The woman thrust a sheet of paper at Nancy and spoke in a mechanical voice.

"Here, complete this form. Return it to me, and then you can take your seat over there with those other people."

"Oh, please, I—"

"As soon as you've completed all the forms, I'll put you on the list to see a doctor. Those are the rules."

Nancy could see that it was hopeless. Silently she filled out the forms and sat down.

The next hour was the longest one she'd ever lived through. Try to relax, Nancy told herself— but she couldn't make herself sit still. She paced restlessly back and forth, watching other patients come and go and listening to the maddeningly calm voice of the woman at the admissions desk.

At last a nurse came to the door with a sheaf of papers in her hand. "Nancy Drew?" she asked.

"That's me," Nancy said, jumping to her feet.

"Come with me, please," said the nurse, and led Nancy down the hall until they reached a little room in an almost deserted wing. "You can have a seat, dear," the nurse said casually. "The doctor will be along in a minute."

Nancy sat down tiredly and leaned her throbbing head against the wall. In a minute the door swung open and a middle-aged woman appeared.

"Miss Drew? Hello. My name is Margaret Liston. What seems to be the trouble?"

For the first time since she'd read the note, Nancy relaxed. Dr. Liston was a quiet and attentive listener, and as Nancy poured out her story she was suddenly confident that things would turn out all right after all.

"I'm going to order some blood tests immediately," the doctor said when Nancy had finished describing her symptoms. "We'll send them to the pathologist and see what turns up. I'm afraid you'll have to wait a little longer for the results to get here—about an hour."

This time Nancy forced herself to sit still. She knew she might as well get some rest while she could. Grimly she fixed her eyes on the wall clock in front of her.

An hour later Dr. Liston returned. "I've got the lab report here," she said, her face absolutely expressionless. "The news is both good and bad. The good news is that we've managed to identify the family—the general category—of poison in your system."

"And the bad news?" asked Nancy, forcing herself to speak calmly.

Dr. Liston's voice was grim. "The bad news is that we haven't been able to pinpoint the exact poison. And that means we can't prescribe an antidote yet."

"I'll try them all!" said Nancy eagerly. "If you've got a basic idea of what kind of poison it is—"

The doctor shook her head. "Those antidotes

vary too much for us to take that kind of chance," she said. "If we were to use the wrong one and it interacted with the poison in your system . . ." She shook her head. "That's a risk we just can't take."

"This is unbelievable!" Nancy cried. "What am I going to do?"

"Well, you're certainly not going to panic," said Dr. Liston firmly. "We'll work on this until we've got the answer. What I'd like you to do is check into the hospital right away. That way we'll be able to keep you under surveillance around the clock."

"I can't do that, Dr. Liston," Nancy said. "I've got to keep working on this case. If I can track down the poisoner, I'll be able to identify the poison. I mean, the poison wasn't meant for me. Surely whoever the culprit is will tell me what kind it was. . . ."

"I don't think that's a safe assumption," said the doctor quietly.

"But the poison wasn't meant for me . . . !" Nancy repeated, her voice trailing off as she realized how hopeless it all sounded. "I do realize you want what's best for me," she added. "And I'll do anything you ask—short of checking in here. I hope you don't think I'm being unreasonable."

The doctor sighed. "No, I truly don't. After all, if you succeed you'll be saving two lives—yours and the intended victim's. But please make sure to call me every couple of hours. Our lab technicians really are good, and the minute we get an answer from pathology we can treat you. Every second counts—but I guess I don't have to tell *you* that."

Nancy smiled sadly. "No, you don't."

The cold air outside the hospital was unexpectedly refreshing. I'll walk back to the hotel, Nancy decided. A little exercise will get my brain going again.

Firmly Nancy pushed every trace of panic out of her mind as she focused her thoughts. She knew the poison she'd "gotten in the way of" had been meant for Kim. But when had the poisoner's mistake occurred? Nancy had shared some food with Kim, it was true—but only tea and cookies, and both Kim and Bess had had the same foods at the same time. Why hadn't either of them been poisoned?

"And what about the dog?" Nancy suddenly said out loud. A woman walking next to her gave her a startled look and veered away to the edge of the sidewalk.

Chanel must have been poisoned accidentally as well. The Yorkshire terrier had drunk the tea meant for Kim—so the poison must have been in the tea. But again, that was the same tea Bess and Kim had drunk the day before without any ill effects!

At least Nancy could tell the vet that the dog

had definitely been poisoned. Maybe the animal hospital's pathologists might identify the poison.

Nancy had been puzzling over these questions so intently that she hadn't been paying any attention to her surroundings. She looked up now to see that she was on a side street that contained nothing but expensive boutiques—the kind with locked doors, which were only unlocked if a potential customer looked rich enough to shop there.

Nancy knew she had to get back to the hotel quickly, but still she slowed down slightly so she could window-shop for a couple of blocks.

A British leather-goods shop—a Swiss chocolatier—a shop specializing in antique wedding gowns—a high-fashion dress shop named Mystère. Well, *that* was appropriate, anyway. Nancy stopped to look at some of the dresses in the shop window.

Wait! she thought. What's that rack of dresses doing back there?

They were certainly beautiful: short evening dresses with strapless white silk tops above deep-toned velvet skirts in crimson, peacock, and emerald. The contrast in fabric and color was as striking now as—as it had been when Kim had introduced a dress just like them in her last show two months earlier. It had been her first attempt at designing formal wear for adults, and it had been very well received.

But that design hadn't been part of Kim's

ready-to-wear line! It had been intended as a one-of-a-kind garment! What were these dresses doing here?

Nancy decided to inspect them more closely. She pressed the shop's buzzer, and in a minute a gray-haired woman walked to the front of the store. She gave Nancy a quick look—and evidently liked what she saw.

"What can I help you with, my dear?" she asked in an unctuous voice when Nancy was inside.

"I'm just looking," said Nancy.

The saleswoman's face tightened slightly, but in a second it was all smiles again.

"Those are pretty ones over there," Nancy continued, walking toward the silk-and-velvet dresses.

"Yes, those are beautiful. And they'd look just lovely on you, dear," said the saleswoman. "But they might be a little out of your price range— Wait, what are you doing?"

"Just checking the labels," Nancy said. "Kim Daley's one of my favorite designers. These *are* hers, aren't they?"

"I—I believe so, but you'd have to check with—"

"But doesn't Kim always put her *own* label in her clothes?" Nancy asked innocently. "Why do these have a Mystère label?"

The saleslady's smile was very forced. "Did I

say those were Kim Daley's? I must have made a mistake."

"But they *are* Kim's," said Nancy. "They're Kim's design, anyway. Would you mind telling me who your supplier is?"

"Would *you* mind getting out of my store right now?" The saleswoman's mask of cordiality had vanished entirely, along with her slight French accent. "You're not a shopper, are you? Are you on Ms. Daley's staff?"

"Well, you could say I was shopping for information," Nancy said smoothly. "And now I have it. Thank you very much." She unlocked the door and let herself out before the saleswoman could say anything else.

I was right, she thought.

There was only one way dresses like those could have made their way into a store like that. Someone must have stolen Kim's design and copied it. Someone was ripping her off.

And it was probably the same person who was trying to kill her!

Chapter

Eight

THE FIRST THING Nancy saw after she pushed her way through the revolving door into the Hamilton's lobby was a forlorn, hunched figure sitting in a chair near a window. It was Bess. The minute she saw Nancy, she rushed to her and almost knocked her down with the force of her hug.

"Oh, Nancy! I've been so worried!" she gasped. "Y-you're still alive!" Her eyes filled with tears. "Sorry I'm being such a dope," she blurted out. "It's just—just been horrible waiting for you." Bess pulled out a tissue and blew her nose vigorously. "Now tell me *exactly* what's going on," she said. "Are you okay? You look so pale."

"I'm fine, but let's sit down. I'm exhausted," said Nancy. The walk back to the hotel had completely worn her out.

Safely enfolded in a large easy chair, Nancy told her friend as much as she knew about the poisoning. By the time she finished, Bess was in tears again.

"I—I took the note to the police," she said, "but there weren't any fingerprints on it. I couldn't even tell if they believed me, Nan. All they said was for you to call them yourself."

"Don't worry," Nancy said, patting Bess on the shoulder. "What we've got to do is figure out a way to get in touch with the poisoner." She thought for a minute. "I guess the only way to do it is to be straightforward."

Next to the information desk Nancy had noticed a billboard covered with news relating to the upcoming fashion show: schedules showing the times each designer would be previewing his or her spring line, advertisements for limousine rentals and catering services, locations of the nearest parking garages—anything that the designers and their staffs might find helpful. She and Bess walked over to it now.

"Well," Nancy said after she'd studied the board, "this looks like the perfect spot to place a classified ad."

She pulled a piece of paper and a pencil out of her purse and sat down to compose her message.

"See what you think of this," she said to Bess after a few minutes.

Accidents can happen. They're completely understandable. Will whoever gave N.D. that surprise package please contact her as soon as possible. Best meeting place—the Grand Ballroom, 3:00. But deadline—*deadline*—is seventy-two hours. All replies confidential.

"It seems fine to me," said Bess. "But I don't like the idea of your meeting with this person, though. Aren't you worried?"

"Of course I am," said Nancy. "But we'll be in a very public place. Anyway, what choice do I have?"

"None." Bess sighed.

Nancy checked the clock. It was almost two o'clock. "Let's hop into the Palm Court and grab some lunch before it closes," she said.

Bess just stared at her. "You can eat at a time like this?" she asked.

"Isn't that usually my line to you?" Nancy rejoined with a smile. "This is not the time to stop taking care of myself—and, anyway, I need to see if Kim's in there. I've got some interesting news for her."

Kim *was* in the restaurant. She was sitting at

her favorite corner table with a subdued-looking Morgan. Kim had her back to Lina's table, where Lina was sitting with Paul and Alison. Even if Kim couldn't see them, Morgan could and kept darting nervous glances at the table.

"Well, the whole gang's here," Nancy murmured to Bess. "Just what I was hoping for." And she strode over to Kim.

"There you are!" Kim greeted her. "I've been looking all over for you! Where *were* you this morning?"

"Oh, I had some things to do," Nancy said vaguely. "Listen, Kim. I passed a store on Colchester Street called Mystère—do you know which one I mean?"

"I think so," said Kim. "The stuff they carry isn't too interesting, but it's well made."

"Especially what they're selling now. You're not going to like this—but someone's been ripping off your designs. They have a whole rack of silk-and-velvet dresses like the one from your last show. Whoever copied it did an awfully good job, too."

Kim stared incredulously at her. "But that dress is one of a kind!" she protested. "You must have made a mistake!"

"I didn't," Nancy said simply. "They're definitely copies."

"My design's been *stolen?*" Kim yelled. "Who's the thief? I tell you, I can't take much more of this!"

A sudden hush fell over the restaurant. Crimson with embarrassment, Morgan muttered, "Kim, don't you think—"

"Don't you tell me what to think!" screeched Kim. "Can you imagine what it feels like to have your work stolen from you?"

Well, this is just what I wanted. *Everyone* knows about the theft now, Nancy said to herself. And there are a lot of suspects in this one room. Paul, Lina, Morgan, Alison— Let's see what happens.

But the results were more dramatic than Nancy had bargained for. Before she could turn to scan the room, Kim had stalked over to Lina's table.

"You did it! You've always wanted to ruin me!" she screamed.

"Miss! Please! Think of others!" The maître d' had arrived at Lina's table almost as quickly as Kim. Sweating profusely, he tried to take Kim's arm, but she shook him off.

"Kim—" Paul began.

"You shut up, Paul! I bet you're in on this, too!"

"Don't bother, Paul," said Lina forcefully. Her face was pale—whether from anger or from fear, Nancy couldn't tell. "Kim knows I wouldn't waste my time on her designs. Don't you, darling?"

Kim's mouth twisted with rage. She took one step forward and grabbed Lina by the throat.

"I'll shake the truth out of you!" she screamed.

Horrified, Nancy got up to rush to Lina's table—but her legs were too weak to hold her. She fell back into her chair just as Paul pried Kim's fingers away from Lina's throat.

"Oh, be careful, Paul!" Alison wailed. "She'll hurt you, too!"

"I'm okay," Paul grunted. Panting, he took both of Kim's hands and pressed them down hard on the tabletop.

"Get hold of yourself, Kim," he said in a very calm voice. "What's the matter with you?"

Kim took a deep breath—and, miraculously, relaxed. "I'm sorry," she said. "I don't know what got into me."

"I should think not!" the maître d' said indignantly. "I'm afraid I'll have to ask—"

Kim wrenched her hands free from Paul's grasp and grabbed Lina by the shoulders. "I'm not through with you, you thief," she said through gritted teeth.

Lina reached up and slapped Kim full in the face. "I'm no thief," she said. "You're just a sore loser. You can't stand the thought that I'm becoming a bigger success than you, can you? Don't bother," she snapped at the maître d', who'd been making futile little noises of protest. "I'm leaving. I can't be bothered with her." With one swift gesture she shook Kim's hands off and rose. Then she walked out of the room.

Not a customer in the restaurant was even

thinking about eating. The waiters were standing still. Everyone was staring avidly at the scene being played out—everyone except Nancy.

She was trying to think why Lina's voice sounded so familiar. It was something about the way she said the letter *s*. "S-s-sore loser" . . . "succes-s-s-s-s" . . . The words had a whistling kind of sibilance that Nancy had heard very recently. . . .

The telephone call to Kim. That was where. Lina's normal speaking voice sounded nothing like the voice on the phone—but now that she was upset, the similarities were obvious.

Lina's the poisoner! Nancy thought. And if I don't get to her soon, she'll be my murderer!

Chapter

Nine

GRADUALLY THE RESTAURANT quieted down as the diners returned to their meals and hushed conversations. Lina had left, Paul and Alison following after her, and a waiter had quickly cleared their table as if to erase any trace of them. Kim had stalked out, too, with a mortified-looking Morgan in tow. But Nancy didn't notice any of this.

"Nancy? What's the matter? I mean, what are you thinking about?"

Nancy turned to face Bess. She'd been concentrating so hard that she'd almost forgotten Bess was there at all. "It's the poisoner," she said quietly. "I think I've figured it out. Bess, it's—"

"Nancy! I've been looking all over for you!"

Nancy turned eagerly. "Ned! Oh, Ned!" she gasped, flinging her arms around him as he rushed toward her. "Oh, I'm so glad to see you!"

"I'm glad to see you, too," said Ned. "I worried about you for the whole drive. And I practically had to knock the desk clerk down to get a room here. Nancy, what's going on?"

"Ahem. I don't want to intrude," said Bess delicately, "but shouldn't we talk about this somewhere else? Like back in our suite?"

"Good idea," said Ned. "Here, let me take your hand, Nan. You don't look too good. Are you feeling okay?"

"I'll tell you upstairs," Nancy said grimly. She was feeling weak and shaky again, and it took all her strength just to keep walking.

When the three of them reached the girls' suite, Nancy collapsed gratefully onto her bed. Ned sat on the bed next to her. "Now, tell me," he said.

Nancy sighed. "Ned," she said haltingly, "I've gotten myself into a horrible situation. I don't know what I did—or what was done to me—but I've been poisoned. The hospital hasn't been able to identify the poison yet, and it's deadly. If they can't come up with an antidote—or if I can't find the poisoner on my own—I'll die in less than forty-eight hours."

As she told him the story, every bit of color

drained out of Ned's face. He opened his mouth to speak, but no sound came out.

"Don't look like that!" Nancy said quickly. Seeing him so scared only frightened her more. "I know I can find the poisoner—especially now that you're here. I get these attacks of weakness once in a while, but the rest of the time I feel pretty good. We'll have to work fast, of course."

Without a word Ned leaned forward and lifted her into his arms, and at his touch Nancy's resolve broke down and she burst into tears. "Ned, this is so awful," she whispered into his chest. "I always knew I loved you, but I never knew how much until I—I knew I might never see you again—"

Ned cleared his throat. "I love you, too," he said in a husky voice. "And we're going to lick this. I won't let you leave me—you'll see." He hugged her hard, then sat up again. "What can I do to help?" he asked, handing her his handkerchief.

"And me?" Bess asked. She sounded as though she was trying to make her voice as bright as she could. "Don't leave me out, you lovebirds."

"Unfortunately, I don't really know what any of us can do," Nancy said wryly. "Well, there is one thing. Ned, you could make two calls for me—one to Dr. Liston, just to see if they've come up with anything, and one to the animal hospital." Nancy knew that Ned had to take some kind of action.

81

As he began dialing, Nancy fell back against the headboard and closed her eyes. In a few minutes Ned hung up dejectedly. "Nothing," he said. "The hospital still hasn't found anything, and neither have the vet's pathologists. But they don't—they don't expect the dog to make it."

"Oh, Nancy!" Bess whispered.

"Let's not even think about that," said Nancy resolutely, sitting back up again. "We've got something else the three of us need to work on. *How* did I get poisoned? Bess and Kim have eaten the exact same foods I have, and they're both fine. I mean, I realize that there are other ways for poisons to enter the bloodstream than from foods, but—"

"What do you mean?" asked Bess. "What other ways?"

"Well, poisons can enter the blood directly— the way they do from a snakebite," Nancy explained. "But nothing's bitten me, I don't have any puncture wounds—"

Suddenly she stopped. "The pin," she whispered. "The pin on Kim's dress! It pricked me when I tried the dress on!

"Bess, help me remember," Nancy said. "When did I first start feeling sick?"

"During lunch in the Palm Court," said Bess. "I'd been taking Sarah to get her cut fixed up, and you'd just come—"

"From Kim's studio," Nancy finished triumphantly. "Where I'd tried on that outfit. It's got to be the pin!"

"And Lina was wearing one just like it," Bess pointed out. "I wonder if she's involved?"

"I'm sure she is!" Quickly Nancy described what she'd noticed about Lina's voice at lunch. "So all we have to do is—"

Then her face fell. "Oh," she said disgustedly. "Lina's not the only person who has a pin like Kim's. So does Morgan. Remember? Morgan was right here when Kim found out about it."

"Maybe Morgan and Lina are in this together," Ned suggested.

"Maybe. Or maybe Paul's the only person involved," Nancy said. Her head was spinning. "He saw me wearing the dress to lunch with Kim. He could have realized then that I'd been pricked and sent me the letter to warn me."

"Slow down," said Ned. "How did the poisoner know you'd get pricked? Am I missing something?"

"The pin was left unclasped, and the odds are good that anyone would prick herself closing it. It probably wouldn't take much of a prick. At least that's what I'm guessing," Nancy explained.

"We could make a case for Paul for sure," Bess continued. "You know, the jilted boyfriend— and speaking of jilted, what about Alison? She obviously worships Paul. Maybe she wants Kim out of the way!"

"I still think Lina's our culprit," Nancy said, picking up the thread, "but we can't eliminate any other suspects yet."

"I wish we could," said Bess.

Nancy smiled slightly. "Well, there's more than just poisoning going on here," she said. "There was that exploding paperweight— remember? That seems like an inside job to me. And then we have the copies of Kim's designs at Mystère. Phone calls—bombs—poison—*and* design theft? That's a lot of activity for one person!"

"So what you're really saying is that there could be more than one mind at work here—and that pretty much everyone whom Kim knows is a suspect," Ned commented.

"That's about it, Ned," said Nancy. "That's about it."

She stood up decisively. "Well, it's almost three—time for me to meet the mystery poisoner. That is, if he or she saw my note."

"Do you want us to come?" Bess asked nervously. "As backup?"

"Actually, Bess, I think you could be more helpful if you'd get that pin from Kim and take it to the hospital," Nancy said. "Tell Dr. Liston about it."

"I'm gone," Bess said. "I'll just get my coat."

When Bess had left, Nancy turned to Ned. "Hey," she said softly, giving him a sad little smile.

"Hey, yourself. What do you want *me* to do, sleuth?"

"Well, I want *you* to come with me. I could use your kind of backup."

"Let's go," said Ned. He bent down and kissed her. "When this is all over," he said, "we're going to have the biggest celebration we've ever had."

"I can't wait," said Nancy.

This was the first time the Grand Ballroom had been empty since Nancy and Bess had arrived at the hotel. Work crews had been there almost constantly, setting up for the show: floodlights were installed; a runway was built; and row upon row of chairs were brought in. Now, though, the place was empty like a stage set before the show. Nancy felt as though she and Ned had just walked onto some kind of nightmare stage. The opulence of the ballroom's high, ornately carved ceilings and parquet floor contrasted strangely with the stark racks of lights and huge speakers hung on the walls waiting to blast out loud rock music. There was a sense of hushed expectancy in the room, as if everything had been set up just for this meeting between Nancy and her poisoner.

"It's three now!" she whispered to Ned. "I mean, it's three now," she said aloud. "Maybe whoever it is didn't see my note at all!"

Just then a side exit door opened—and Paul Lavalle walked in—Alison Haber directly behind him.

"Hello, Paul," Nancy said quietly. Her heart was racing and her palms were damp, but she wasn't going to let him know how nervous she was.

"Nancy!" Paul said genially. "Boy, that was some scene at lunch, huh? What a bunch of crazies we hang out with. What are you doing here, anyway—auditioning for a modeling job?"

"Hardly," Nancy answered, her tone icy. "Let's not waste time on small talk, Paul. You know I've got to hurry."

Paul stared at her. "Whoa! I'm totally confused. Alison, is it just me?" He grinned at Lina's assistant.

"You know what I'm talking about!" Nancy said. "Please, Paul! If all I did was get in the way, then you've *got* to tell me what kind it was!"

"What kind *what* was?" Paul asked after a second.

"Please stop this! You saw my note, didn't you? Why else would you be here?"

"Note? Nancy, I'm just here to check out the lights."

"Stop jerking her around, champ!" Ned burst out angrily. "We both know you poisoned her."

"Ned, please! I can handle this," Nancy whispered. Turning to Paul—who now looked completely stunned—she said, "The person who accidentally poisoned me was supposed to be here at three. And here you are. It seems like a pretty funny kind of coincidence to me."

"You're insane!" Alison cried. "Paul wouldn't do something like that!"

Paul spread his hands helplessly. "What can I say? She's right. I mean, I wouldn't do something like that—and if you think I did, you *are* insane."

"I think that what happened is that you saw me and got cold feet," Nancy said evenly.

"Sure I've got cold feet!" Paul snapped. "I'm surrounded by crazy women these days. The only one who's not jumping on me is Alison! I've had enough! I'm out of here!" And he strode angrily toward the door.

Ned blocked his way. "Where are you going?" he asked. "You try to kill my girlfriend—and then you call her crazy?"

"Ned!" Nancy said. "Calm down!"

"I see that both of you are crazy," Paul said airily. "Get out of my way, Captain America."

"I'll get you out of *my* way!" Ned shouted.

And he hauled off and punched Paul in the stomach with all the strength he had.

Paul keeled over without a sound. His head hit the floor with a thud.

Alison gave a terrible scream. Sobbing hysterically, she rushed over to Paul and threw herself down beside him.

Then she looked up at Ned, her face a ghastly mask of grief and horror.

"You've killed him!" she shrieked.

Chapter

Ten

NANCY BENT DOWN to take Paul's pulse, but her fingers were too stiff to close around his wrist, and she was trembling.

"You murderer!" Alison screamed at Ned. Her eyes were slits of hatred.

Ned was staring aghast at Paul. "I—I don't know what came over me," he stammered. "I never meant to—"

Nancy tried to speak, but there was something wrong with her voice. Suddenly the room was spinning around her. Faster and faster it whirled. Spots of bright red and yellow danced in front of her eyes, and waves of nausea washed over her with sickening speed.

I'm falling, Nancy thought to herself just before she hit the ground.

As if from miles away she heard Ned calling her, but she couldn't even lift her lids to look for him. Velvety blackness swooped her up and carried her away. . . .

"It was all just too much for her, I guess," came a familiar voice. "She hasn't—hasn't been feeling well, you know."

Nancy opened her eyes. "Hi, Bess," she said weakly. "What are you doing here?"

"I got worried. I came looking for you, and I heard screaming," Bess said. "You fainted just as I was running in the door."

Then Nancy remembered what had just happened. "Paul!" she gasped, struggling to sit up. "And Ned! Where are—"

"Paul's okay," Bess said quickly. She put an arm under Nancy's shoulders and lifted her up. "I mean, at least he's not dead. I called an ambulance. See, they're just getting him now."

Two paramedics were lifting Paul gently onto a stretcher. Alison was hovering over him, tears streaming down her cheeks.

"Why can't I come with you?" she asked rebelliously. "I won't get in the way, I promise!"

"Sorry, miss," said one of the paramedics

sympathetically. "Really, it'll be easier for everyone if you stay here. You can call the hospital to check on his condition, and I'm sure they'll let you visit. Besides, don't the police want to question you?"

What police? Nancy turned quickly—and almost fainted again. Two officers, standing at the main entrance to the Grand Ballroom, were putting Ned in handcuffs.

"Ned!" Nancy gasped.

He tried to move toward her, but the police officers held him back. "Take it easy! You're not going anywhere," one of them told Ned gruffly. "Except with me." The two of them began to lead Ned out the door.

"Don't worry, Nancy!" Ned called back over his shoulder as he was pulled away. "Get some rest. I can handle this alone!"

He waved at her—and then disappeared around the corner.

"No! I've got to come, too!" Nancy cried. Before Bess could stop her, she had struggled to her knees. But another wave of faintness washed over her, and she sank back to the ground again.

"I can't believe you want to go with him," Alison said tearfully as Bess helped Nancy to a chair. "When he practically murdered Paul just for walking into this room! We're not here because we saw that stupid note! We just came in because we had work to do."

"If I've made a mistake, Alison—believe me, I'll be sorrier than you," Nancy said wearily. "Bess, could you help me upstairs? I really don't feel well."

"Of course, Nan. Here—give me your hand," Bess said. "We'll have you back upstairs in no time."

It seemed like ages to Nancy, but at last she was back in bed in her room. "Ohhh," she groaned as she relaxed against the pillow. "I can't believe how awful I feel. What time is it?"

"Quarter to four," said Bess.

Nancy groaned again and closed her eyes. The whole horrible thing had taken less than an hour. Less than an hour for Ned to be arrested, for one of her prime suspects to be sent to the hospital, for Nancy's confidence to be completely shredded. If Paul hadn't seen the note on the bulletin board, had anyone?

"Did you get the pin?" she asked Bess, her eyes still closed. "Please tell me something positive for a change!"

Bess sighed. "I can't. It's missing. Kim and I looked everywhere for it, and we couldn't find it. I'm sorry, Nan."

"Great," Nancy said. "That's all we need, isn't it?"

"There's one more thing," Bess said hesitantly. "Nan, the vet called Kim. Chanel's dead. She died at three this afternoon."

Nancy winced. "Poor little thing," she said. "Poor Kim, too. She really loved that dog." She shivered. "And if Chanel died so quickly, what does that say about my chances!"

There were tears in Bess's eyes. "Don't talk about that!" she begged.

"I'm going to try not to think about it—not until I've had some sleep, anyway. If I don't get a nap, I'll never be able to keep going."

"I'll get out of here right now. How about if I come back in an hour?"

"That'd be fine," Nancy said sleepily.

When Bess had left, Nancy turned over and buried her face in the pillow. But the sleep she was longing for didn't come right away. No matter how desperately she wanted to, she couldn't shut out her thoughts.

Who was the poisoner? Her very life depended on the answer to that question.

There was Paul, who owned the voice distorter, and who had shown up at the wrong spot at the right time. There was Lina, with her strange speech impediment and her imitation version of the poisoned brooch. And there was Morgan, with dozens of reasons to hate Kim—and an imitation brooch of her own.

Those cheap imitations were just like the imitations of the one-of-a-kind dresses Kim had designed. Too many suspects—too many copies. Were they all implicated?

There was one more suspect, Nancy reminded herself—Alison. Alison had been at the Grand Ballroom at the right time, too. She was crazy about Paul—so much so that it didn't seem impossible that she might want Kim out of the way. Was there any chance that she was the poisoner? It didn't seem likely—but neither did anything else about this case.

Nancy finally felt groggy again and snuggled into the pillows to fall asleep.

It seemed like only minutes before Bess was shaking her gently. "You'd better get up if you don't want to sleep straight through till morning," she said.

"Thanks, Bess," Nancy mumbled. "Did you call the hospital? Has my dad called?"

"Yes, to the first question; no, to the second. The hospital is—is still working on it, but I'm sure they'll come up with the antidote soon. No word from your dad. And someone taped this to your door," Bess added.

"This" was a cream-colored envelope, and the sight of it instantly jerked Nancy awake. Her heart pounding, she reached out and took the envelope from Bess.

The typeface was just the same as on the other anonymous note Nancy had received.

"I thought so. My friend's back," Nancy said grimly. She handed the note to Bess.

" 'Now I know that you deserve to be poisoned

just as much as Kim does,'" Bess read aloud in a shaking voice. "'You can forget about the antidote, too. You're just as bad as Kim is, and you'll die just the same way she will. I'll get you in the same ways I mentioned in my letters to her.' Oh, Nancy! What are we going to do?" she wailed.

"Wait a minute. Wait a minute," Nancy said rapidly. "There's something that doesn't fit here. If I weren't so sleepy, I'd— Wait, I know what it is! Kim *hasn't* been getting threatening letters! She only mentioned phone calls!

"Boy, this case makes me want to pull out my hair," Nancy added. "Maybe there are two people involved—one who's been making phone calls and one who's been trying to poison Kim."

"And don't forget the stolen designs," Bess reminded her. "Maybe there are three criminals."

"Well," Nancy said bitterly, "I guess all we have to do is eliminate the people who aren't suspects. That'll make things a lot simpler."

"Don't talk like that, Nan," said Bess. "I know you can figure it out. At least Paul's out of the running for this note," she added, brightening. "He's in the hospital."

"That's true. I guess he's not the letter-writer, so he's probably not the poisoner, either. I'm starting to think that Morgan put the poison on the pin. And the pin and the exploding paper-weight seem like inside jobs to me. Maybe Lina stole the designs. . . ."

"How?" Bess asked blankly.

"Bess, let's just take one thing at a time," Nancy said with the first smile she'd smiled all afternoon. "And let *me* get out of bed," she added. "This definitely isn't one of those cases that can be solved from an armchair."

She dragged herself out of bed and stumbled into the bathroom, where she turned the cold-water tap on full blast and began splashing her face. Is it just my imagination, she asked herself, or is the poison already starting to make me look different? In the mirror her eyes appeared huge and sunken, making them look haunted, her face thin and pale. Well, there was only today and tomorrow left. . . .

Don't think about it! Nancy ordered herself. She snapped off the faucet and walked back into the bedroom.

"Before I do anything else, I've got to find out what's happening with Ned," she said to Bess.

Nancy shook her head and dialed the local precinct. "He must really have snapped," she said, "or he'd never have attacked anyone. I'm almost sorry I called him. Hello? This is Nancy Drew. I'd like to get some information about someone who was brought in for questioning earlier. . . . His name? Ned Nickerson. Has he been released yet?"

"Released? When he's been charged with assault and battery?" said the gruff voice at the other end. "He's not going anywhere—unless it's to jail!"

Chapter

Eleven

CLICK! THE LINE went dead before Nancy had a chance to say anything.

"When are they releasing him?" Bess asked as Nancy hung up the phone and sat down.

"They aren't," Nancy said in a dull voice. "They're charging him with assault and battery." Tears filled her eyes. She brushed them away angrily. "Sorry—it's no use my getting upset. I just feel bad for Ned. He'd never have gotten into trouble if he hadn't been worried about me. Oh, I hate this case!"

"Nancy," Bess said logically, "Ned's only been charged with assault and battery, and he wouldn't want you to waste time worrying about him now. He'd want you to keep trying to solve the case so you can find the antidote. And that's what I want, too."

"You're right, of course," said Nancy, wiping away the stray tear that had escaped down her cheek. "Thanks, Bess."

Bess leaned forward and gave Nancy a quick hug. "Sorry for being bossy, Nan. But we need you to keep thinking clearly. You can let me be the mushy, emotional one if you want."

"All right," said Nancy with a smile. "I'll do that." She jumped to her feet. "Let's start thinking about which suspect we want to see first," she said briskly as she paced back and forth. "Paul's temporarily off the scene, of course. I'm sure Alison's with him. Lina's preparing for her show, so we can't talk to her now. And that leaves Morgan Daley. You know, Bess, we actually don't know much about Morgan except how horribly Kim treats her. I think I should speak to her."

"Want me to come?" Bess asked.

"No, there's no reason. You just relax for a while, and I'll meet you back here when I've finished talking to Morgan."

But finding Morgan turned out to be easier said than done. First Nancy had to talk to Kim—and Kim was in a terrible mood.

"What did the hospital say about the poison?"

she asked the minute Nancy walked into her office.

"Nothing yet," said Nancy. "They've been in touch with pathology labs all over the country, but they still haven't been able to identify it."

"Great," Kim snorted. "So I guess we just sit around and wait for you to die, too?"

The expression in Nancy's eyes must have given Kim pause. She reddened and turned away. "Sorry," she said. "It's just been a horrible day."

"I'm sorry about your dog," Nancy told her sincerely, and there was a long silence.

"Do you have something to tell me?" Kim finally asked.

"Well, actually, I have something to ask you," Nancy said. "I'd like to have a word with your sister. Do you know where she is?"

"The hotel pool, probably," said Kim. "I gave her a break, and she always tries to get in some exercise when she can." She sounded as though she considered that a personal fault of Morgan's. "But what does my sister have to do with anything?" Kim went on. "You don't think *she's* involved with this, do you?"

"I'd just like to talk to her," Nancy said carefully. "At this point we can't rule anybody out."

Kim smiled a little scornfully. "I suppose you mean I've got a lot of enemies," she said. "Well, that's the way it is when you're on top."

Once again Nancy was silent. How could you talk to someone like Kim?

"Try the pool," Kim said again. "She's probably there. And tell her to get back up here when you're done with her."

"When you're done with her?" Nancy repeated to herself as she got into the elevator. Kim makes it sound as though I'm on my way to beat Morgan up!

Nancy could smell the chlorine at the entrance to the pool. She leaned against the heavy door and walked in.

There was only one person inside the dimly lit pool—Morgan. She was doing solitary laps, stroking hypnotically through the water with a grace she didn't have on land.

She didn't notice Nancy, or she pretended not to. She just kept swimming steadily back and forth. At last Nancy went and stood next to the aluminum ladder leading up out of the pool.

This time—as Morgan turned her head out of the water to breathe—she did see Nancy. Her eyes widened, and she turned her head away as she kept swimming. But now her movements were choppy and awkward.

She knows I'm watching her, Nancy thought. "Morgan!" she called. "I really have to talk to you. Could you come out now?"

"Just let me finish this lap," Morgan gasped back over her shoulder. As she came closer to where Nancy was standing, she began to swim more and more slowly, and when she finally began to pull herself out of the water, it was as if her whole body shrank away from Nancy.

Nancy couldn't wait any longer. *I don't know if this strategy will work,* she thought, *but I've got to try it. She's hiding something, and I've got to find out what it is!*

"Morgan, I know all about it," she said. "And I think you're in over your head. Come on—tell me the truth."

Fear flashed like lightning across Morgan's face, and she froze with her hands on the ladder. "Okay. I—I'll tell you everything," she whispered. "I'm so sorry—"

Suddenly Nancy relaxed. It was going to be all right at last! "Thank you," she said, and she meant it from the bottom of her heart. "But could you give me the antidote first?" she asked.

Now Morgan looked confused. "Antidote? Wh-what antidote?"

"You mean you don't *know* what the antidote is?" Nancy asked.

"I don't know what you're talking about!" Morgan hadn't said it indignantly; she sounded genuinely bewildered. And all of a sudden Nancy was absolutely convinced that Morgan *didn't* know what they were talking about.

"Morgan, someone poisoned me by mistake," Nancy said. "It was your sister they were after."

"You've been poisoned? *Poisoned?*"

"Yes. Just like Chanel—only I'm pretty sure

101

the poison was on that ruby pin Kim designed. I pricked myself with it. And now I've only got about a day and a half to find the antidote."

Morgan pushed herself up the ladder. Still staring at Nancy, she walked as if in a trance to a nearby bench. She picked up a towel and began drying herself. Her eyes still hadn't left Nancy's face.

All right, thought Nancy. I believe that you didn't poison me, Morgan. And there we go with another one-step-forward, two-steps-back development in this case. Feeling utterly defeated, Nancy sank down onto the tile floor and put her head on her knees.

Suddenly she lifted her head again. "Morgan," she said, "you were about to tell me everything. Everything about what? What did you think I was talking about?"

"About Lina, of course," Morgan said simply. "I thought you'd found out about her somehow."

"Found out what?" Nancy asked.

Wrapping herself in the towel, Morgan walked over and sat down next to Nancy. "I was so afraid you'd find out about this," she said with a sigh, "and now it seems like nothing at all compared to the fact that you've been poisoned. I let Lina inside Kim's workshop about ten days ago."

A sob shook Morgan's body. "I was so angry at Kim. She'd been screaming at me all day about something that I'd had nothing to do with, and she'd bawled me out in front of the whole staff. Not that that's anything new—it just seemed worse than usual that day. So when Kim went out to dinner and left me there alone—and when Lina came to the door and said she just wanted to look for a book of models she'd lent Kim—I decided to go ahead and let her. I even went into another room while she was in Kim's office. I knew I shouldn't have let her in, but I just didn't care."

She gave Nancy an anguished look. "And she must have been trying to *kill* Kim! And now you might die because of my stupid mistake! I'll never forgive myself! Never!"

"But think how much your telling me this has helped," Nancy said comfortingly. "Now we know that Lina is probably the poisoner. But wait, how long was she in there? How could she get hold of the pin, apply the poison, and put the pin back on the dress without your seeing? She must be incredibly confident."

"I—Wait! Now that you mention it, she *couldn't* have done it!" Morgan said incredulously. "Not during that visit, anyway. I was in the workroom with her all the time. She was only alone for a minute in Kim's office. The designs for the dress and the pin were in the workroom, and the dress was at the presser's—with the pin on it."

"The presser's? What's that?" Nancy asked.

"That's where we send all our new designs

after they're finished," Morgan explained. "Any new design has to be pressed before it's worn— and you have to use a professional presser. Our fabrics are so expensive that we can't risk trying to iron them ourselves."

"What's the name of your presser?" Nancy asked excitedly. At last there was a development in the case that might lead somewhere!

"He's Rafael Orsini," said Morgan. "Most of the top designers in Chicago use him."

"So it's possible that Lina—or whoever the poisoner is—got into Orsini's shop and poisoned the pin there?"

"Yes," Morgan said. "It's completely possible." Unexpectedly she smiled. "You don't know how relieved I am, Nancy. If I'd had to spend the rest of my life knowing Lina had applied poison to that pin because of my mistake . . . I can't even think about it."

"Of course she must have been doing *something* in there," Nancy said.

Morgan's face hardened. "Yes—and now I know what it was. A few days after I let Lina into Kim's office, she said she had a present for me. It was a copy of Kim's design for the ruby pin. I knew it was an imitation of Kim's design, but I took it anyway. I thought it was very nice of her to think of me," Morgan said scornfully. "She must have stolen the idea when she was in the office."

"And she gave you the pin to brag that she had stolen it," Nancy put in.

Morgan shivered suddenly. "I should really go and change," she asked. "I'm freezing, and the pool will start getting crowded in a few minutes. It always does at dinnertime."

"Sure," said Nancy, getting to her feet. "And then maybe you can tell me how to get to Mr. Orsini's shop. Will it still be open?"

"Until six-thirty. But are you sure you should go right now?" Morgan asked. "You do look awfully pale."

And I *feel* awfully pale, Nancy thought. "I can't take a break now, Morgan," she said. "I just can't. But I do appreciate all the help you've given me. Truly, you've been more helpful than anyone else I've talked to so far."

"I'm glad. And, Nancy, good luck. I mean it."

Nancy smiled. "I'll keep you posted," she said.

"Of course I'll come with you," Bess said a few minutes later. "Let me just grab my purse." She darted into the adjoining room.

I'm so tired, Nancy thought. I've never been so exhausted in my life. And my head is pounding. If I could just get some air . . .

She trudged over to the window and wrenched it open. A welcome blast of fresh air filled the room. Nancy sat down on the windowsill, breathing in the cold gratefully.

And in that split second dizziness hit her like a tidal wave. With a sickening lurch her body swayed sideways, and before she could catch herself—before she could even scream—she was falling backward out the window toward certain death.

Chapter

Twelve

NANCY GRIPPED THE SILL with her knees and hung on by sheer force of will. Only her calves and feet were still inside the window, but they were slipping now. The blood was pounding in her head as she made an attempt to raise her hands back to the window ledge. But her body would not respond to her brain's command.

"Bess . . ." she moaned, and the wind snatched her words away. "Help me. . . ."

"Nancy! Oh, no! I'm coming!"

Bess flew to the window and grabbed Nancy by the knees. She held on and slowly hoisted her friend back into the room as easily as if she'd been George or Ned. Together they lay on the floor in a heap.

Finally Bess raised herself up on her elbow. "I can't leave you alone for one second," she joked shakily. "Who do you think you are? Superwoman?"

Nancy was breathing too hard to speak. What if I'd come up here alone? she kept wondering. "Thanks, Bess," she panted at last. "You saved my life! If you hadn't been there . . ."

"Well, I was," Bess said, patting Nancy's shoulder. "Let's—let's not even think about it. Oh, Nancy!" There were tears in Bess's eyes, but in a second she straightened up resolutely. "Okay, enough emotion," she said lightly. "This is your slave driver speaking again. Let's head on over to Orsini's before he closes."

"That means another visit to Kim's suite to get directions," Nancy said reluctantly. "But you're right, Bess. Let's go."

Luckily Kim was too busy to pay them much attention when they got to her office. She was intently studying a striking six-foot-tall model dressed in a scarlet metallic tube-top dress with what looked like matching biking shorts beneath. Her assistant Sarah was standing next to her with a pen and pad, prepared to take notes.

"Did you find my sister?" Kim asked abstractedly when they knocked on her office door.

"Yes, and she was very helpful," Nancy replied. "But now I've got to bother you for something else—the address of Mr. Orsini's shop."

Kim turned to stare at Nancy. "Surely you don't suspect Rafael?" she asked incredulously. "He's a sweet old man."

"No, no," said Nancy. "We just want to ask him a few questions." She grinned. "I bet you've heard me say that enough."

Kim didn't smile back. "Here's the address," she said, scribbling it down on an old envelope. Then she turned to the model again.

"The hemline's crooked," she said to Sarah. "And, Carlotta—"

The beautiful model gazed anxiously at Kim, and suddenly Nancy recognized her. She'd last seen her on the cover of *Glamour*.

"I know you're a hot new model," Kim said icily, "but please remember what you're doing. That dress is for teens. It's supposed to be fun. So look as if you're having *fun*, for heaven's sake!"

Carlotta looked completely crestfallen. "Yes, Miss Daley," she murmured, plucking nervously at one of her sleeves.

Nancy caught Bess's eye, and they started for the door. But they were stopped by Kim's voice.

"So you're still not making any progress, Nancy?"

Nancy looked her straight in the eye.

"On the contrary. We're actually making very good progress," she said. "I'll definitely solve this case, but I'm not sure you'll be happy with the results. You really do have a lot of enemies, you know." And she walked quietly out the door with Bess.

Rafael Orsini's tailor shop was only a few minutes away by taxi. It didn't look as imposing as Nancy had expected. In its window, a dusty-looking mannequin modeled a red suit straight out of the 1950s, and a small sign on the door read simply, R. ORSINI—LUXURY TAILORING.

"I hope he's still here," said Bess. "It's after six, you know."

"He will be," Nancy replied. "Until six-thirty."

As soon as Nancy and Bess opened the door, they were hit by the loudest flamenco music they'd ever heard. It made the whole shop shake.

But where was everyone?

"Hello," called Nancy. "Anyone home?"

Behind the counter was a drawn curtain. Nancy saw a bell on the counter and picked it up and rang it, then rang it again.

She was sure that no one would be able to hear the slight tinkling sound above the music, but to her surprise, a tiny man dramatically stepped out from behind the curtain the second time she rang. He couldn't have been more than five feet tall, and he had a precise, fastidious appearance—a small mustache, gray hair parted in the middle, a neat blue suit, and gold spectacles. Nancy found herself smiling down at him.

"Mr. Orsini?" she asked.

"You're looking at him. What can I do for you?"

"My name is Nancy Drew. I'm a private investigator—"

Immediately Mr. Orsini stepped back in feigned horror, his eyes twinkling. "So young?" he exclaimed. "And such a pretty girl to be doing such dangerous work."

"It's not a joke, Mr. Orsini," Nancy said in a low voice. "I'm working for Kim Daley—and what I'm about to tell you must be in strictest confidence. There's been an attempt made on her life."

Mr. Orsini looked horrified. "That beautiful woman? So gifted? Who would want to—"

Then his voice wavered, and he looked away, biting his lip. He must know what her reputation is, Nancy thought. Maybe he's even witnessed her temper firsthand.

"There's more to it," she went on. "We have reason to think that someone is stealing Kim's designs—or trying to. What kind of security measures do you have here?"

Mr. Orsini's eyes widened in surprise.

"*Security?* At Luxury Tailoring? We have never had a problem. And not only that—I know everyone in the business! Chicago is really a small town when it comes to fashion. There aren't that many people in the business, and I know them all personally."

"Well, is there any chance that someone—a competitor, say—could have sneaked in here and gotten hold of Kim's designs?" Nancy persisted.

"Impossible. Absolutely impossible. We don't let anyone but employees into our workroom—not ever."

Hmmm, thought Nancy. "Does Kim have any clothes in the shop now?" she asked.

"Let me see . . ." said Mr. Orsini. "She did this morning, yes, but she was planning to have the clothes picked up today, I know. Let me call my assistant and see whether someone's already come by for them. Miss Swang!" he called. "Turn down the music and come out here for a second!"

The music stopped, and a sudden silence hung in the air. What a strange-looking woman! Nancy thought as Miss Swang pushed her way out through the curtain. That's got to be the worst haircut I've ever seen! It looks as though she cuts it with a scythe!

Miss Swang's hair just hung there, lifeless and somehow dusty looking. And the clothes she was wearing seemed to have been chosen at random —an electric-blue polyester shirt, a dark green wool cardigan, a red corduroy skirt, and expensive-looking alligator shoes.

"You wanted me, Mr. Orsini?" she asked in a hoarse, grating voice that was painful to listen to.

"I did, dear. These two charming young ladies would like to talk to you. Miss Swang is a part-time assistant here," he explained. "I always take on extra help before a big fashion show. Have Miss Daley's clothes been picked up today, Miss Swang?"

"Let me check the records," Miss Swang croaked, picking up a notebook. "Yes, they have," she said after a second.

"Do you know who pressed them?" Nancy asked. Maybe a word with the presser who'd handled Kim's clothes would turn something up.

But Miss Swang's answer was disappointing. "No one in particular," she said. "I mean, all the pressers work on all the designs. We don't make assignments or anything."

She turned to her employer. "Do you need me for anything else?"

"No, thanks, dear," he answered.

Miss Swang pushed her way back through the curtains, and in a minute the music began pounding away again.

Mr. Orsini spread his hands apologetically. "You see," he said, "as I said, nobody comes in here off the streets. Except you two. Everything is by appointment, and I know everyone." He broke off and gave Nancy a penetrating stare. "What exactly are you looking for?" he asked.

"There's one outfit we're especially interested in," said Nancy. "It's a pearl-colored silk suit with a cropped jacket and a knee-length skirt. It's got a ruby brooch on the jacket. Do you remember it, Mr. Orsini?"

"I certainly do," he answered emphatically. "But I did not work on it. Let me get the slip for you to see." He pulled out a box of receipts and began leafing through them.

"Is it unusual for your customers to leave jewelry on their clothes?" asked Nancy. "I assume you take the brooches off before you clean or press them—"

Mr. Orsini drew himself up to his full height and glared at Nancy as though she'd insulted him. "Of course we do," he said. "And our customers know they can trust us! My assistants are instructed to list any jewelry that is left on the clothes and then lock the piece in the vault."

Nancy and Bess were studying the slip. "But there's no mention of a brooch on this slip," Bess said. "Isn't that strange?"

"Then perhaps there was *no* brooch," said Mr. Orsini. "Why do you keep asking about this pin? Is there one missing?"

"Yes," Nancy said. "It's missing *now*. It wasn't taken from here, we know, but we want to know what happened to it while it was here. That's why we want to know who might have handled it."

Mr. Orsini still looked ruffled. He shrugged his shoulders impatiently. "My staff is reliable," he said. "If you do not believe that, there is no way I can *make* you believe it."

"I'm sorry to have upset you," Nancy said. Another dead end, she thought to herself, disappointed. "Would you do me a favor? If you do hear anything about the brooch, would you call? It's—it's more important than you know." She could feel herself beginning to wilt again.

Bess was watching Nancy anxiously. "I think it's time to get you home, Nan," she said.

"All right," Nancy said exhaustedly. "Let's go, then. Thank you, Mr. Orsini."

Now the little man's face was filled with concern. "You are not well?" he asked. "I didn't realize it."

"Of course she's not well!" Bess burst out indignantly. "That pin she's been asking about was—"

"It's all right, Bess," said Nancy. "Let's just go get a cab. Thank you, Mr. Orsini."

Out on the street Nancy stood shivering in the cold while Bess hailed a taxi. "So what do we know?" she asked once they'd settled themselves in the cab. "Nothing more than we knew before."

Bess patted her shoulder comfortingly. "Don't give up, Nan," she said. "There's still a—still most of a day left—" Her voice broke, and she turned her head to stare out the window.

As the girls crossed the hotel lobby to the elevator, more than one head turned to watch them. We must look pretty strange, Nancy thought. Bess is practically dragging me along. But Nancy was too tired and disheartened to care what anyone thought.

"I remember you locking the door, Bess," she

115

said when they reached their floor. "Or was I supposed to do it? Now I can't remember."

"I *did* lock it," Bess said.

"But look!" Nancy whispered.

A tiny sliver of light was shining through the crack. I *know* we turned the lights off, Nancy thought. And even if we hadn't, the only way we can see any light through the door from here is—is if it's open!

"Stay here, Bess," Nancy murmured. She tiptoed up to the door, her eyes wide.

"It's unlocked!" she whispered to Bess. "And I can hear someone inside!"

Chapter

Thirteen

THERE'S TROUBLE behind that door, thought Nancy. And I'm in no shape to deal with it.

But I have to. She took a deep breath, stepped forward, and shoved the door open.

"Ned!" she gasped.

He was stretched out on her bed. Now he sprang to his feet and took her in his arms.

"It's *Ned?*" Bess shrieked from behind them. "Ned! Don't ever do that to me again! I almost had a heart attack!"

"Sorry," Ned said with a grin. "I didn't mean to scare either of you. I thought I'd closed the door." He leaned over and switched off the TV,

which he'd been watching with the sound off. *"I
was the one who was scared. When I got back
here and no one answered the door, I got worried. For all I knew you could have been—
unconscious or something. So I used that old
credit-card routine you showed me once, Nan—
and opened the door. I guess I half expected to
see you stretched out on the floor."*

"Well, I didn't expect to see *you* at all," Nancy
said. "When did the police let you go?"

"About an hour ago. I'm so sorry I lost my
temper with Paul." He grimaced. "I guess 'lost
my temper' is kind of a mild way to put it. I still
don't know what came over me. I was just so
worried about you, and I thought he'd been the
one who'd poisoned you, and, well, I lost my
head. The worst thing about it all was thinking
how much extra trouble I'd made for you."

"Well, you're back," said Nancy, kissing him
on the cheek, "and that's what's important. And
you only did it because you cared for me—so I
can't really get too upset."

"And Paul's okay," Ned added. He smiled a
little. "It turns out he passed out from nerves, not
from being punched. Anyway, he's not pressing
charges."

He put his hand on Nancy's chin and lifted her
face. "How are you?" he asked gently. "That's
the only important question."

Nancy met his eyes steadily. "Not great," she

said, "but Bess has been taking incredible care of me. When we have time, I'll fill you in."

"Don't bother," said Bess. "But I do think you should go to bed now, Nan. You need some rest. You can start work again in the morning."

"I agree," said Ned.

"I don't," said Nancy. "There's just not enough time! Once I find the antidote I can rest. I've got to talk to all the suspects again—tonight, if I can." *I'll have plenty of rest if we don't find the antidote,* she added grimly to herself. *I'll have nothing but rest.*

Something of the sort must have occurred to Bess and Ned, too. "By the way, I called the hospital for you, Nancy," said Ned after a little silence. "They're—they're still working on it."

"Well, where would you like to start?" Bess finally asked, breaking the silence that followed Ned's report.

"With Lina," Nancy answered immediately. "And this time we're not leaving until we get some answers."

It was only a few seconds in the elevator and a few steps from there to Lina's suite, but by the time they'd reached the door Nancy's legs were buckling under her. Ned and Bess had to support her—one on each side.

There was the door. To Nancy's tired eyes it seemed to quiver as she knocked.

No answer. "Well, it *is* late," Ned pointed out.

"She must have left." He tried the doorknob—and it turned easily in his hand.

Ned swung the door open, and the three of them peered into Lina's suite. "No sign of life," Bess said. "Should we come back later?"

Nancy's lips were a thin line. "No," she said. "It's even better if she's not here—if no one's here." She reached past Ned and switched on the light. "I want another look at that voice distorter. And you two can poke around to see if there's anything here that looks like one of Kim's designs. I know we're snooping, but detectives just have to *be* snoops once in a while."

Lina's workroom seemed a mile long as Nancy slowly made her way across it. And she'd only gotten halfway there when her head began to swim again. She staggered over to Lina's sleek, streamlined desk and eased herself into the chair.

There were papers strewn all over the desk, but Nancy was too tired to focus on any of them. There could be a whole stack of stolen designs here, she thought, and I wouldn't be able to see them. What a great detective I am. . . .

She swiveled in the chair until she was facing Lina's typewriter. A single sheet of paper was in the machine, and Nancy stared at it idly—the letters swimming in and out of focus.

Then she sat up straighter in the chair and concentrated to steady the words. The sheet of paper was a letter. And it was addressed to Bronwen Weiss.

Bronwen Weiss . . . Who *is* that? Why is that name so familiar? Nancy wondered. Then she remembered. Bronwen Weiss was the Chicago *Tattler's* gossip columnist—the one who'd trashed Kim so badly in the paper the day before. Why was Lina writing to her?

Nancy squinted and leaned in closer to the letter. Gradually she began to realize why Lina had written this letter.

Dear Bronwen:

Kim Daley's at it again. What some designers won't do for publicity. *She's* the one behind all those rumors that someone has been making death threats to her. Can you believe it? She even poisoned her own dog to make the whole thing more believable! I know it sounds incredible, but I was there at the time. And it doesn't stop there. She's hired a private detective to look into these "threats," just so her story will be more convincing. It's pretty sad, really. All this fuss just to take away attention from the fact that her show's going to be so pathetic. . . . Hope this will come in handy for your column.

The letter ended there.

I wonder if Lina was planning to put her own signature on this, Nancy thought. I bet she wasn't. "Hey, gang," she called in a low voice, "come and look at this."

After Ned and Bess both read the letter, Ned asked, "Who's Bronwen Weiss?" And Bess said, "Pretty nasty stuff."

"Her last column just about butchered Kim," Nancy said, "and none of us could figure out who'd tipped Bronwen off. I guess Lina must have been the source for that one, too."

Ned shook his head. "So this is the glamorous world of high fashion!" he said sarcastically. "When you have competition, you just find some junky tabloid and spread a few rumors. Makes me glad I'm just a humble college student."

"Does this mean Lina's the poisoner?" Bess asked. "If she hates Kim *this* much . . ."

"I don't think so," Nancy answered. "Who'd bother to write a poison-pen letter when they were using real poison? I mean, it's the difference between calling someone a name and stabbing the person! Lina hates Kim—but Lina's a pussycat compared to whoever dipped that pin.

"I *do* think Lina made those threats over the phone, though," she added. "She's got that voice-distorting equipment over there"—Nancy pointed to the corner—"and she also has that speech defect that the vocoder couldn't hide. Besides, nasty phone calls and nasty letters seem —seem to go hand in hand. . . ."

It was an effort for Nancy to get the words out. Her body felt heavy and made of clay, and she could hardly keep her eyes open. Ned was talking now, but he sounded as if he were down a well.

"Lina will probably be back any moment now. Do we wait and hit her with our big guns or what?"

"No," Nancy said feebly. "The trouble is, we still don't have any clue about the poisoning." She shook her head despairingly. "If Lina's not the one, and if Morgan isn't the one, and if Paul isn't the one—then who's left?"

Nancy wobbled to her feet. "I've got to get back to bed," she muttered. "Can you guys help me?"

She was concentrating so hard on not falling over that she didn't see the panicky look Ned and Bess exchanged as they rushed to her side.

"Ups-a-daisy! Here we go!" Ned said cheerfully, lifting her. But his face was white with worry.

Once she was up in her room, Nancy fell into bed fully clothed. Nothing Ned or Bess said could reach her, and the world of high fashion meant nothing to her now. There was only one thought in her mind as blackness overcame her.

She had just half a day to live.

Chapter

Fourteen

W<small>HEN</small> N<small>ANCY</small> <small>WOKE</small> <small>UP</small>, sunlight was pouring through the windows. Bess was sitting in a chair next to her bed, reading a magazine. "You're awake at last," she said, smiling. "I woke up really early—couldn't sleep—and came in here. I wanted to keep an eye on you."

"Thanks, Bess," Nancy said with a yawn. She stretched, sat up, and looked at her travel clock. It was seven!

"Bess, what's the matter with you? Why did you let me sleep so late?" cried Nancy. "This could be my last day! There's no time left!"

"I—I'm sorry, Nancy," Bess stammered. "I

just thought you needed lots of sleep so you could get your strength back. I guess I wasn't thinking."

Nancy forced herself to relax. None of this was Bess's fault, after all. She took a deep breath and slowly got out of bed. *"I'm* the one who's sorry," she said, giving Bess a quick hug around the shoulders. "I shouldn't snap at my best friend.

"I'll call Dr. Liston," she added, "and then we can get going."

Dr. Liston wasn't in her office, so Nancy had her paged. As she waited, she couldn't help imagining how wonderful it would be if the doctor's news was good. She'd rush down to the hospital, get the antidote—then have a huge, celebratory reunion with Ned and Bess. Then she'd call Hannah and tell her about the narrow escape she'd had. It would be like waking up from a bad dream, and her friends would all be wide-eyed as she told them the story.

"Hello, Nancy?" came Dr. Liston's voice. "I was down in the lab. Nancy, my news is not good."

"Oh, no." Nancy closed her eyes and slumped against the wall. From her chair by the bed, Bess watched her in alarm.

"We've made no progress since yesterday," said Dr. Liston. "And we've got to have the identity of the poison before midmorning so we can prepare the antidote in time. Is there any chance of that?"

"I hope so," Nancy said in a tiny voice.

"I'll be here by the phone from now on," the doctor promised. "And, Nancy, even if you don't find the poisoner in time, please come to the hospital. Even if we don't have the antidote, we can—we can at least make you more comfortable than you'd be in the hotel."

"Make you more comfortable"? She means they'll help me die more comfortably! thought Nancy, appalled. "I'll come," she said aloud. "One way or the other, you'll see me there."

When she hung up the phone, something inside Nancy's head clicked into place. This was it. There was no more time for self-pity and no more time for panic. She was losing energy faster and faster—but if the next few hours were going to be her last ones, she'd at least go down fighting.

"I'm going to grab a quick shower," she told Bess, "and then we can get going."

First Nancy made the water as hot as she could stand it. Then, to rinse off, she turned on the cold tap full blast. The icy needles of water were pure torture, but when Nancy stepped out of the shower, she felt wonderfully refreshed. There was a knock at the door just as she finished dressing. Nancy opened it and found Ned there. Like Bess, he looked drawn and haggard, and Nancy's heart contracted with pity. He's taking this even worse than I am, she thought. But if I had to stand by helplessly and watch *him* die . . .

"Come in," she said gently, taking Ned's hand and pulling him into the room. "You're just in time for breakfast."

"Shall I call room service?" asked Bess.

"No way! We're going to the Palm Court," Nancy replied.

"No way yourself!" said Bess. "You're not going to run all over this hotel. I don't want you wasting energy like that."

"Wasting energy? I can't *do* anything up here," Nancy retorted. "We're going to the Palm Court for breakfast. And then I'm confronting every suspect on the list. Okay?"

Bess looked up at Ned. "Do we do what she says?"

"She's the boss," Ned answered lightly. He looked as though he was fighting to keep a smile on his face.

"Then we're off," said Nancy. It was just seven-thirty.

"Wow," Nancy murmured as they walked into the Palm Court. "Doesn't this place ever empty out?" The restaurant was as crowded and clamorous as it had been at lunch. Kim—dressed in a Day-Glo green minidress and Day-Glo orange stockings and white boots—was conspicuous in one corner as she dictated something to Morgan. She nodded briefly as they passed her table.

"They must all be having breakfast meetings," said Ned.

"Well, that's what we're going to have, too," said Nancy. She had just spotted Paul Lavalle at a table across the room. "There's the first person I'm going to meet with." And she hurried across the room to his table.

Paul was buried in the morning paper. He jumped when Nancy tapped his shoulder—and frowned when he realized who it was. "What do you want *today?*" he asked sarcastically. "Is a mass murderer supposed to be sitting at this table?"

"Oh, Paul, I'm so sorry for what happened yesterday!" Nancy answered. "I still can't believe it myself. Please believe me when I say that it was all a terrible mistake."

"A little more than a mistake, I'd say," Paul answered shortly.

"You're right, of course," Nancy said. "I only wish I could make it up to you somehow. If I could explain everything— Can you possibly join us for breakfast? There's a lot to talk about."

"Is your boyfriend going to jump me again?"

"Oh, Paul, Ned feels awful about what he did—he's never done anything like that before. He went wild because he thought you had tried to kill me. Can't you understand that?"

"I guess so," said Paul slowly. He stood up, beckoned to his waiter to bring the order to Nancy's table, and followed Nancy back to where Bess and Ned were sitting.

Ned stood up quickly and held out his hand when he saw Paul.

"Hey, I'm really sorry," he said, turning a little red. "I hope Nancy explained. And thanks for not pressing charges against me."

"Forget it," said Paul with a wave of his hand. "What can I do for you all?"

Their first course arrived just then, but Nancy didn't touch her melon. Instead she pushed it aside and laid her hands on the table.

"I'll get right down to it, Paul. Why didn't you want me to see that voice-distortion equipment?"

"That's been bothering you?" Paul asked, a note of real surprise in his voice. "No mystery there! It's just a theatrical device—I'm planning to use it for Lina's show. I kind of liked the idea of introducing each new outfit with a different voice. I just didn't want Kim's people to find out about it, that's all—I was afraid they'd steal the idea."

"How could they steal the idea if they didn't know about it?" asked Bess.

"Well, you and Nancy were hanging around with Kim," Paul said. "I was afraid you might talk, that's all. That's *really* all."

"But you got so angry so fast—"

"Well, I could hear Lina in her office. You weren't supposed to know she was there. I wasn't sure if she could hear us—but I wanted to make it absolutely clear to her, if she *was* listening, that I wasn't doing anything to hurt her interests."

"Okay, but what about the fact that you just happened to be in the Grand Ballroom at the time I'd arranged to meet the poisoner there?" asked Nancy. "You have to admit *that* looked suspicious."

"I admit it! I admit it!" said Paul, half laughing. "But it really was just a coincidence—they do happen every once in a while, you know. I was just there to check a few things." He rubbed his stomach ruefully where Ned had punched him. *"That'll* teach me not to be compulsive about my job."

"And it'll teach me not to jump to conclusions," said Nancy with a sigh. "Maybe you can help me, though. While you were in the ballroom, did you see anyone else there?"

"Let's see . . ." Paul thought about it while Nancy took an unenthusiastic bite of her melon. "No," he finally said. "It was just me and Alison. She did seem a little ill at ease, but then she always does. She's kind of a nervous person, I guess."

Around you, anyway, thought Nancy, but she didn't say it.

"Well, speak of the devil!" Paul said genially. "Here's Alison herself! Maybe you can ask her if she saw anyone. Hey, Alison! Good morning!" He gave her a cordial wave as she walked toward their table.

But Alison didn't look especially cordial that morning. "I thought we were having breakfast together—just you and me," she said with a toss of her short blond hair. She hadn't even glanced at anyone else at the table.

"Well, there's plenty of room here," Nancy said. "Won't you join us?"

Alison still wouldn't look at her. "No, thanks," she said briefly. "I'll sit over there." She pointed to a table in the far corner of the room. "Paul, would you come over when you're through?"

She turned and began to weave her way through the crowd.

She's probably not a suspect, Nancy said to herself. After all, she must be able to see that Paul's not interested in her the way she is in him. But I have to check *everyone* out today, even the most remote possibility. . . .

She jumped up quickly and began to follow Alison across the room. But she never made it. The air around her suddenly began to shimmer and pulse in front of her eyes—and Nancy fainted.

"Let me through! Let me through!" It was Ned's voice that brought Nancy back to consciousness. But where was he?

She lay on her side in a dreamy haze. I'm just not going to get up this time, she thought, and closed her eyes again. It's too comfortable here.

"Please, will you let me through?" shouted Ned again from the back of the crowd.

Nancy's eyelids fluttered open. "Don't bother, Ned," she murmured. "I'm fine right here."

All she could see were feet. Feet stood in a circle around her: a well-burnished pair of men's wingtips; a pair of black pumps with gray stockings; dark green snakeskin boots; and an elegant pair of women's alligator shoes.

Wait a sec, Nancy thought drowsily. I've *seen* those alligator shoes before.

Where had it been? Nancy couldn't remember. She was about to close her eyes again when it suddenly hit her—and jolted her awake.

At Mr. Orsini's tailor shop. His strange assistant Miss Swang had been wearing them. They had stood out because the rest of her outfit was so weird—

Nancy stiffened on the floor. A new idea had just flashed through her mind.

Mr. Orsini had said that no one could get at the clothes in the pressing company because security was too tight. But what about someone who already worked at the pressing company? An employee would have access to all the clothes, of course! And what if an enemy of Kim's had applied for a job there? It would have been simple for that person to poison Kim's brooch!

Finally, what if that person had made one tiny mistake—the mistake of wearing the same shoes

132

at the pressing-company job as she did at her job in the fashion world?

Then whoever wore those shoes would be the poisoner.

And that meant that the poisoner was right there in the crowd surrounding her!

Chapter

Fifteen

ALL THIS had flashed through Nancy's mind in an instant. Now, abruptly, she raised herself up on her elbows—and met Alison's gaze.

Alison! Nancy darted a look down at the girl's feet. yes. It was Alison who was wearing the alligator shoes. She must have been wearing a wig and different makeup at Mr. Orsini's—but Nancy was sure now that Miss Swang was none other than Alison herself.

She's the one who poisoned me!

Time froze as Nancy looked up slowly into Alison's eyes again. They held a sudden terrified awareness.

She knows that I know, Nancy thought. And the words came out before Nancy knew what she was saying.

"Alison, it's you," she gasped. *"You're* the poisoner!"

With a strangled cry Alison spun around and crashed her way through the crowd.

Nancy struggled to sit up, but she was too weak. "Someone stop her!" she cried. "She's a murderer!"

Ned finally broke through the circle of people and reached down to pull Nancy to her feet.

"Are you all right?" he asked.

"Don't think about me!" Nancy said frantically. "You've got to catch Alison!"

As she turned in the direction Alison had run, Nancy saw that Paul was already chasing her with Bess a few steps behind him. And from their separate tables across the room, Kim and Lina rose to their feet and followed, too.

Ned grabbed Nancy's hand and pulled her through the restaurant so fast that her feet barely touched the ground.

"They're going into the Grand Ballroom," Nancy panted. "Hurry!"

They burst through the door—and stopped short.

Someone had turned on all the spotlights in the room. They beamed an intense, merciless light onto the models' runway. In a few days some of the world's hottest models would be sweeping down that runway—but there was only one person on it now. Alison.

She was cringing like a trapped animal under the blinding lights in the middle of the runway, her hands held out in front of her as if to ward off an attack. And Kim, Paul, Bess, and Lina were slowly, menacingly advancing toward her.

"So *you're* the one who tried to kill me! You little worm!" hissed Kim. "You're not going to get out of this one. They're going to put you away forever!"

"She's crazy!" Alison said tremulously. "Help me, Paul!"

"*Help* you?" Paul repeated incredulously. "Why would I do that? You tried to kill the woman I love!"

Alison burst into tears. "It's not true," she sobbed. "Tell me it's not true! You *don't* love her!" She turned away and buried her face in her hands. "You're acting like some kind of lynching party!" she cried.

"It's better than you deserve," Kim snapped.

"Stop, everyone!" called Nancy. "Stay where you are! It's okay. She's not going anywhere."

She walked haltingly toward the runway, trying to conceal how weak her legs were. Her eyes were fixed on Alison. "No one's going to hurt you," she said. "But it's all over, Alison. I don't know why you did it—and I don't care. All I want is—"

"Well, I care!" Kim interrupted savagely. "She's a—"

"Please!" Nancy said. "I need some information from this girl right away!" Spots were starting to dance in front of her eyes again.

"You need information? I'll give you information!" said Lina. "She tried to blame this all on me! She gets no sympathy from me, I'll tell you that much!"

"Or from me," Bess chimed in. "Nancy, she tried to *kill* you!"

Nancy lurched as a shudder racked her body. *"Stop,* everyone!" she said, and they fell silent. Nancy looked straight into Alison's eyes. "I've got your poison in me," she said. "And if you don't tell me the name of it, I'll be dead before lunch."

Carefully she climbed the stairs to the runway and put a hand on Alison's shoulder. "No one's going to hurt you," she said again. "We just want the truth."

A shudder wrenched Alison's entire frame, and she pulled away from Nancy's touch. Her fists were clenched, her face beaded with sweat. But suddenly she relaxed. And when she began to talk, the light in her eyes looked almost angelic.

"I've always loved Paul," she said. "When he was working with Kim and I was just starting out with Lina, I saw him everywhere. Mostly, people ignored me, but Paul was always so nice to me!

He always asked me how I was doing, he always said hi when he saw me. . . ."

"Sure he did," said Kim. "He felt sorry for the ugly duckling."

Alison stared into Paul's face and smiled beatifically. "I know that's not true, Paul," she said. "I *know* you really cared about me. You were the only person who asked me how I was doing. You took a real interest in me. And that's why I love you."

Kim snorted incredulously, and Nancy gestured fiercely that she should be quiet. But Alison didn't seem to have noticed—except that now she turned her gaze on Kim.

"I hate you, Kim," she said in the softest of voices. "You were *using* Paul—using his infatuation with you to get every drop of blood out of him. He thought you loved him—but I knew better. You're the kind of woman who's only in love with her career.

"So I decided that I should get you out of the way," she continued simply. "This world doesn't need more people like you. And that way, I'd have a better chance with Paul."

Nancy glanced over at Ned. He looked as horrified as she felt.

"I guess you know what happened next," Alison said to Nancy. "In a funny way, it was all Morgan's idea. She once told me how careless Kim was with the jewelry she designed, and how

Morgan was always having to retrieve it from places like the presser's.

"So I got that part-time job at Mr. Orsini's— and waited. I knew I'd get the chance to use that poison sometime. I wasn't sure how, but everything comes if you wait long enough, doesn't it? And my chance came when Morgan brought in that new outfit Kim had designed—and forgot to take the brooch off. Perfect!" Alison chuckled. "I realized right away that Lina had copied the brooch—I'd seen the drawing in her office—and that meant that Lina had been alone with the brooch at some point. So I figured Lina'd get the blame if anyone did. And if somehow no one thought of Lina, there was always Morgan. . . ."

Nancy cleared her throat. She was having more and more trouble speaking—each word took a huge effort. "But I got in your way when I tried the dress on unexpectedly, didn't I?" she asked.

"You sure did!" Alison said. "At first I felt terrible when Paul mentioned that you'd worn it. But when you tried to kill Paul"—she stared accusingly at Ned—"I decided not to help you anymore." She shook her head. "I still hadn't had any luck with Kim, though. I put the poison in her sugar when room service left a food cart outside her door—and then she *still* didn't get any."

Kim gasped, but Nancy's warning look stopped her before she said anything.

"Where's the pin now?" she asked.

"Oh, I sneaked in and threw it out once I'd realized what had happened," Alison said airily.

"So you—so you sent me that second letter," Nancy prompted. She could hardly see now; the pain in her head was so bad. Ned glanced at her anxiously, but she didn't notice. "And you mentioned those threats Kim had been receiving. That's where I started to get confused, Alison. You said you'd do all the horrible things to me that Kim had read about in those anonymous letters. But she'd been getting telephone threats, not letters!"

Alison sighed. "I guess I blew it there. When I read about the threats in Bronwen Weiss's column, I just assumed they were coming in letters." Then she brightened. "Well, so I made one mistake! It doesn't add up to much when you think how many mistakes I *didn't* make."

"Until this morning," Nancy said quietly, "when you wore the same shoes you'd worn at Mr. Orsini's."

"Right. Until this morning. That was really—" Alison broke off and shook her head.

"Well, it's all over now," Nancy said. "And now you won't be charged with murder. You can give me the name of the poison, and I'll go right to the hospital." If I get there in time, she said to herself. If I can just hold on a little longer . . . But she didn't think she'd be able to hold on.

So this is what it feels like when your life ebbs away, she thought.

Alison just stood there. There was a smile on her face as if she hadn't quite understood what Nancy was saying.

"Tell her what the poison is!" Bess cried.

Alison didn't seem to hear Bess. She was still smiling at Nancy. "You're right," she said. "It *is* over."

She pulled a white handkerchief out of her pocket and pressed it against her lips. For a second she stayed upright—and then her eyes rolled back in her head. She coughed a little, stumbled backward, and fell to the floor.

Shock galvanized Nancy into action. In an instant she was beside Alison, tearing away the handkerchief from the girl's mouth. There on Alison's lips was a yellowish substance—some kind of powder. Nancy bent to look at it more closely. Then, horrified, she reeled back.

"It's the poison!" Nancy cried. "She's poisoned herself."

She grabbed Alison's shoulders and shook her. "Tell me the name of the poison!" she pleaded. "I've got to know!"

There was no answer. Alison was only half conscious. Her head lolled sickeningly to one side, and she sagged like a limp rag doll in Nancy's arms.

The only person who could save Nancy's life was dying!

Chapter

Sixteen

FRANTICALLY NANCY TURNED to Paul. "She loves you!" she cried. "You've got to help me save her. It's my only chance!"

Without a word Paul scrambled up onto the runway and knelt at Alison's side. He took a deep breath—and picked her up in his arms.

"Alison, it's me—Paul," he said hoarsely. "Don't die! I do care about you!"

He shook her gently, then more vigorously. "Someone get some ice water," Nancy gasped over her shoulder, "and call an ambulance!" Immediately Bess dashed out of the room.

Paul took Alison's chin in his hand. "I don't want you to die," he said frantically. "Everything's going to be all right, Alison. Kim is still alive. Nancy is still alive. Tell me the name of the poison. You don't want to be responsible for the death of an innocent person, do you? Please, Alison. Save your own life. You have too much to live for!"

Bess came running back in with a pitcher in her hand. "Here's the ice water," she panted. "Ned's calling the ambulance."

Paul grabbed the pitcher and splashed a little of the water on Alison's face. And now at last she began to stir. She moaned, and a garbled stream of words came out of her mouth. The little circle of people watching her pressed closer.

"Alison, talk to me!" Paul begged.

"Nothing to . . . live for." Alison sighed. "Want . . . to die."

"No!" said Paul. He shook her again. "*I* don't want you to die! Hey, come on, who will I take to breakfast if you're not here? Who will I complain to? Come on, Alison. I care about you!" His voice broke. "I really do," he added, almost to himself.

Outside Nancy could hear the wail of an ambulance. The siren cut off abruptly, and then there was the sound of feet thudding toward the Grand Ballroom. "They're here," she said to Paul.

143

Alison gave the ghost of a smile and murmured something no one could hear.

"What was that?" Paul asked, bending down toward her.

Alison smiled again—a peaceful smile, as if she'd somehow finished struggling. She whispered something into Paul's ear.

"Thank you," Paul said fervently. "We've got it, Nancy!" he shouted. "She told me the name of the poison!"

The ambulance attendants were rushing into the room now. Nancy held her hands beseechingly up to Ned. "Help me," she said.

He scooped her up in his arms. "It's okay," he whispered into her hair. "You're going to be all right now—and you solved the case. I love you, Nancy."

But Nancy was too weak to answer.

Dr. Liston was waiting for them all at the hospital's emergency entrance. A flurry of hospital attendants descended on Nancy and Alison, and rushed them into the building.

"Get them up to pathology right away!" ordered Dr. Liston. "I only hope we're not too late," she added, looking anxiously down at Nancy's face.

Nancy hardly heard her. She was barely aware of being rushed through the corridors as doctors and nurses raced beside her gurney.

"I think we're losing her," Dr. Liston said

quietly to a nurse. "If that antidote's not ready within the hour, it's all over."

Nancy woke up and stretched luxuriously. Only a day had passed since she'd been brought here, but she felt like an entirely new person. The white sheets around her felt wonderfully crisp, and the huge bouquet of flowers in the vase next to her bed gave a sweet scent to the whole room. Even the drab green walls looked beautiful this morning.

In fact, Nancy thought with a grin, I love everything about being here—green walls, IV drip in my arm, ugly hospital gown, everything. I'm *alive!*

"Knock, knock," said a warm voice at her door, and a beaming Dr. Liston walked in. "Looking good, I see," she said approvingly. "You're a great patient, Nancy. We'll be able to discharge you very soon. I'd like to keep you under observation for a few more days, but I'm sure there'll be no problems.

"Gorgeous flowers," she added. "Who sent them?"

"I think Ned did," Nancy said. "The minute you told him I was going to be okay." She could hardly remember anything of what had happened the day before, but she did remember Ned's jubilant face when he and Bess had finally been allowed to see her at the end of the day.

"He was awfully happy." Dr. Liston smiled at

the memory. "You know, we had a rocky couple of hours when it looked as though there wasn't going to be time. When I finally went into the waiting room and told your friends we'd finished —and that it was working—I thought they'd yell the place down."

"How *is* Alison doing?" Nancy asked.

A shadow crossed the doctor's face. "As well as can be expected. She took a lot of poison—much more than you got, of course—and swallowing it made it work much faster than your dose did. We almost lost her, and she's still very weak. But she'll live to stand trial. What ends up happening to her is all a question of whether or not she understands what she did.

"Now, you're meeting with everyone who was involved in the case this morning, right?" the doctor added.

"Right," Nancy said. "Bess arranged it. I just wanted to fill them all in. And I think I hear them coming now."

"Nancy?" Bess peeked into the room. Behind her were Ned, Paul, and Kim.

"Come on in," said Dr. Liston. "I was just leaving. Have a nice visit, but don't stay too long. We don't want the patient getting tired out." She winked at Nancy and went out the door.

"Sorry there aren't more chairs," said Nancy as her four visitors filed in.

"That's okay," Kim said brusquely. "I'm not staying long."

She walked up to Nancy's bed and stared down at her, expressionless. "I just want to say one thing," she blurted out. "I know about Lina stealing my designs. Morgan told me she'd let her into my office. And she—she kind of blew up at me. She really let me have it. I guess I'd never realized how much she hated the way I treated her."

Kim looked down and began fidgeting with her hands. It was strangely unsettling to see her so ill at ease, like looking at a completely different person.

"While Morgan was talking I suddenly realized how—how important she is to me," Kim continued. "It's not only the business part of it, although I see now that I couldn't possibly manage that side of things without her. It's more—well, even when I've been horrible to her, she's always been loyal to *me*. Letting Lina into my office was the only time she ever went behind my back—and I have to admit I can't blame her for having done it."

She glared down at Nancy. "So I gave her a raise and promised I'd make it up to her. And now I'll say what I really came here to say. I hate apologizing, but I apologized to her. And I'm apologizing to you, too. You saved my life, and I'm going to try to live it like a better person from now on. Thank you."

Kim turned and marched out the door.

"Wow!" Bess said after a second. "She didn't

even mention the fashion show once! She *must* have decided to change her life."

"The show's still on, though," put in Paul. "Kim should sail through it—especially now that Lina won't be taking part."

"She won't?" Nancy raised herself up on one elbow to stare at him. "What happened?"

"She confessed," said Paul. "Confessed to stealing the designs and making all those threatening phone calls *and* planting a bomb in Kim's office.

"It's an incredible story," he went on. "Once she'd memorized the designs she saw in Kim's office, she hired a secret partner in New York and sent him drawings she'd made from memory. He took the designs to a sweatshop and had some samples run up overnight, then sent the samples back to Lina. She sweet-talked the owner of Mystère into selling them later. Apparently he didn't question her too closely about where they would be coming from. I gather he owed her some kind of favor. Lina swears it was the first time she'd tried something like this. She was hoping she'd be able to make a little money on the side and steal Kim's thunder at the same time."

"What about the bomb in the paperweight? How'd she manage to get that in, with hotel security so tight?" Nancy asked.

"The U.S. mail," Paul answered. "One of

those gag-item catalogs. The bomb was originally part of an exploding cake, if you can believe that—something you'd order as a party trick. Lina had noticed Kim's paperweight once, and she bought a duplicate. There was a little hollow in the bottom of the paperweight, and she just stuck the bomb in there. She guessed Kim would never notice it with her desk always in such a mess—and if she *had* noticed, what was there to connect the bomb with Lina?"

"Lina certainly knew how to plan ahead," Nancy said dryly.

"She sure did," Paul said. "Knowing her, I'm sure she'll hire some hotshot lawyer—and there'll be a long trial. But no matter what sentence she gets, Lina is ruined in this town. Unless she changes the name of her company to Hot Properties."

Just then Dr. Liston poked her head into the room. "So much for the late-breaking news," she said. "Everyone clear out now. This girl needs her rest!"

"Just one thing," said Bess. "Nan, your dad called last night. He'd made a call home to Hannah—I guess he was having such bad luck catching fish out in the middle of nowhere that he moved to a lodge closer to town—and she told him she thought there was something the matter with you. I filled him in on everything, and he's calling me back today. He wants to know whether you want him to come home."

Beaming, Nancy shook her head. "Tell him to keep fishing," she said. "I'm just fine—and tell him it's mostly because of you. If you hadn't been around to help me—"

"Oh, stop," said Bess, blushing. "All I did was nag you once in a while."

"I'm serious, Bess," said Nancy quietly. "You were the best friend I could have had. You really came through for me when I needed you the most. I'll never forget it."

Bess leaned forward and gave Nancy a big hug. "I'm just glad you're okay now," she said. "Now, Mr. Nickerson," she added sternly, "I'll wait for you down in the lobby. You have five minutes. Don't tire the patient out." As she and Paul walked out, she closed the door gently behind her.

Ned took Nancy's hand and held it tightly. It was a long time before he spoke.

"I'm glad you're alive," he said at last. Then he put his arms around her and gave her a bone-crushing hug.

"Easy! Easy!" Nancy said with a laugh. "I'm a sick woman!"

Then she drew his head down for a kiss. "But I'm getting better all the time," she whispered. "So stick around. We have lots more cases to solve."

Ned collapsed on the edge of the bed, his face filled with mock anguish.

"Oh, no! More cases? When does it end?"

Nancy fluffed up the pillows and settled back in bed.

"It doesn't," she answered with a smile.

Nancy's next case:

Five years ago Lucinda Prado died in a freak boating accident in Tahiti during a storm. Lucinda, a beautiful and successful actress, was married to director Brian Gordon. Now their daughter, Bree, has received anonymous letters hinting that Lucinda's death was not an accident—she was murdered. Bree calls on Nancy to help her.

From the moment Nancy arrives in Tahiti it's clear someone wants her off the case. A deadly sea snake is put in her bed, and someone takes a potshot at her and Bree with a spear gun. Then Nancy uncovers one undeniable piece of evidence—the anchor chain from the Gordons' boat, which was deliberately cut, setting Lucinda adrift. Now the girls are too close to the truth. Nancy is forced into a fierce underwater duel with Lucinda's murderer. And all the while a great white shark is circling for the kill . . . in *TROUBLE IN TAHITI*, Case #31 in The Nancy Drew Files™.